Inhaling deeply, she selfishly enjoyed another tantalizing breath warmed by Chris's skin, perfumed by his masculine scent. Then she pushed herself back to sitting, forcing him to move back and drop his arms.

He studied her intently, his dark eyes boring into hers. "You do know that I'm going to protect you, right? You seem...scared, or maybe worried."

Unable to stop herself, she caressed his face. Her heart nearly stopped when he rubbed his cheek against her hand. Oh, how she wished her life were different, that she had met this man in another place, another time.

He smiled, a warm, gentle smile she felt all the way to her toes.

"Everything's going to be okay, Julie," he said. "We'll figure this out. Together."

"Thank you," she whispered back. Her gaze dropped to his lips, and hers suddenly went dry. She automatically leaned toward him. Her hands went to his shirt, smoothing the fabric.

A shudder went through him and she looked up, her eyes locking with his. The open hunger on his face made her breath catch. And then he was leaning toward her slowly, giving her every chance to stop him, to pull away, to say no.

But she didn't.

MOUNTAIN WITNESS

—

LENA DIAZ

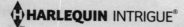
HARLEQUIN INTRIGUE®

Thank you, Allison Lyons and Nalini Akolekar.

For my family…George, Sean and Jennifer. I love you so much.

And in loving memory to the family member who has passed over the rainbow. I'll always love you, Sparky.

ISBN-13: 978-1-335-72081-8

Mountain Witness

Copyright © 2017 by Lena Diaz

Recycling programs for this product may not exist in your area.

Printed in U.S.A.

Lena Diaz was born in Kentucky and has also lived in California, Louisiana and Florida, where she now resides with her husband and two children. Before becoming a romantic suspense author, she was a computer programmer. A former Romance Writers of America Golden Heart® Award finalist, she has also won the prestigious Daphne du Maurier Award for Excellence in mystery and suspense. To get the latest news about Lena, please visit her website, lenadiaz.com.

Books by Lena Diaz

Harlequin Intrigue

Tennessee SWAT

Mountain Witness

Marshland Justice

Missing in the Glades
Arresting Developments
Deep Cover Detective
Hostage Negotiation

The Marshal's Witness
Explosive Attraction
Undercover Twin
Tennessee Takedown
The Bodyguard

CAST OF CHARACTERS

Chris Downing—Part-time SWAT officer, full-time detective, his annual summer bash turns violent when he has to save his new neighbor. Just who is this mystery woman? And is she a witness in hiding, or is she hiding something else entirely?

Julie Webb—After surviving one attempt on her life, she hides out in rural Destiny, Tennessee. But there's more than one killer after her. And the only person who can save her is the one person who doesn't trust her: Officer Chris Downing.

Kathy Nelson—Does the assistant district attorney really want to help Julie? Or does she have far more to gain if Julie is dead?

Brian Henson—Administrative assistant to the ADA, or something more sinister?

Elizabeth Abbott—Estranged grandmother of Julie Webb. What will she do to protect the family's secrets?

Max Remington—Fellow SWAT officer and detective in the Destiny Police Department. Is he trying to help Chris, or settle an old score?

Harry Abbott—A distant cousin suddenly appears from Julie's past. Who is he, and what does he have to do with the attempts on Julie's life?

Chapter One

Blood, there was so much blood. Julie stood over him, one hand braced on the bed's footboard, the other still holding the gun. The blood soaked his shirt, seeping between his fingers as he clutched at the bullet hole in his side. Air wheezed between his teeth, his startlingly blue eyes blazing with hatred through the openings in the ski mask. The same eyes that had once stared at her with such love that they'd stolen her breath away.

Right before he'd said, "I do."

Julie Webb shook her head, blinking away the memories, wishing she could put the past behind her just as easily. Her hands tightened on the steering wheel as she sat in the driveway, the thin pale line on her ring finger the only tangible reminder of the diamond that had once sat there.

Stop it. He can't hurt you anymore. It's time to move on.

Unfortunately, with most of her assets frozen while the courts did their thing back in Nashville,

moving on meant hiding out in the tiny—aka afford-
able—rural town of Destiny, Tennessee. And with
the limited rentals available in Blount County, she'd
chosen the lesser of evils, the one place with some
land around it—an old farmhouse that had sat vacant
for so long that the owner had been desperate to rent
it. Desperate equaled cheap. And that was the only
reason that Julie had taken it. Well, that and the fact
that Destiny was a good three hours from Nashville.
She wasn't likely to run into anyone she knew in the
local grocery store.

The sound of a horn honking had her looking in
her rearview mirror, reminding her why she was in
her car to begin with. The moving truck sat idling
in the gravel road that ran past the expansive front
yard, waiting for her to back out so it could back in.
After two days of living out of a suitcase and sleeping on the floor, having a couch and a bed again was
going to feel like heaven.

She put the car in Reverse, hesitating when she
noticed that her only neighbor had come out onto
his front porch. Long, unpaved road, dead end, sur-
rounded by acres of trees and pastures, and she still
had a neighbor to contend with. A handsome, sex-
on-a-stick kind of guy to boot. Which was going
to make ignoring him difficult, but not impossible.
She'd had her own sex-on-a-stick kind of man before. And look what it had gotten her.

He flashed her a friendly smile and waved just as
he'd done every time he'd seen her in the past two

days. And once again, she pretended not to notice. She backed out of the driveway.

Rhythmic beeping sounded from the truck as it took the place of her car, stopping just inches from the porch that ran along the front of the white clapboard house. It was a much smaller, one-story clone of the place next door. There weren't any fences on either property, so she wasn't sure where his acreage ended and hers began. But clearly he had a lot more land than her rental. The mowed part of his yard extended for a good quarter of a mile to the end of their street.

She didn't care, didn't want to know anything about him. The only way to survive this temporary exile was to keep to herself and make sure that none of her acquaintances figured out where she was. Which meant not associating with the hunk next door or anyone else who might recognize her name or her face, in case any of the news stories had made it out this far. She fervently hoped they hadn't.

The movers had the ramp set up by the time she'd walked up the long gravel driveway. It would allow them to cart the boxes and furniture directly to the top of the porch without having to navigate the steps. That meant everything should go quickly, especially since she didn't have much for them to unload—just the bare essentials and a few things she'd refused to leave in storage.

She risked a quick look toward the house next door. The friendly man was gone. A twinge of guilt shot through her for having ignored him. He was probably a perfectly nice guy and deserved to be treated better. But her life was extremely complicated right now. By ignoring him, by not letting him get involved in any way in her problems, she was doing him a favor.

"Ma'am, where do you want this?" one of the movers asked, holding up a box.

Apparently, the thick black letters on the side that spelled "kitchen" weren't enough of a hint.

She jogged up the steps. But, before going inside, she hesitated and looked over her shoulder at the thick woods on the other side of the road. The hairs were standing up on the back of her neck.

"Ma'am?" the mover holding the box called out. He lifted the box a few inches, as if to remind her he was still holding it.

"Sorry, this way." She headed inside, but couldn't shake the feeling of doom that had settled over her.

Chapter Two

Chris shaded his eyes against the early afternoon
sun and watched through an upstairs window as the
curvy brunette led one of the movers into the house
next door. He didn't know why he bothered waving
every time he saw her. Her standard response was
to turn away and pretend that she hadn't seen him.
He'd gotten the message the first time—she wanted
nothing to do with him. Too bad the good manners
his mama had instilled in him, courtesy of a well-
worn switch off a weeping willow tree or his daddy's belt, wouldn't allow him to ignore her the way
she ignored him.

He leaned against the wall of the corner guest
bedroom, noting the car that his neighbor had parked
on the road. He couldn't remember the last time
he'd seen a BMW. Most of the people he knew had
four-wheel drives. Come winter, that light little car
would slide around like a hockey puck on the icy
back roads. Then again, maybe she didn't plan on

sticking around that long. Summer was just getting started.

A distant rumble had him looking up the road to see a caravan of trucks headed toward his house, right on time to start his annual beginning of summer cookout. The shiny red Jeep in front was well ahead of the other vehicles, barreling down the road at a rate of speed that probably would have gotten the driver thrown in jail if he wasn't a cop himself, with half the Destiny, Tennessee, police department following behind him.

Dirt and gravel spewed out from beneath the Jeep's tires as it slowed just enough to turn into his driveway without flipping over. The driver, Chris's best friend, Dillon Gray, jumped out while the car was still rocking. He hurried to the passenger side to lift out his very pregnant wife, Ashley. Chris grinned and headed downstairs.

He'd just reached the front room when the screen door flew open and Ashley jogged inside, her hands holding her round belly as if to support it. The door swung closed, its springs squeaking in protest at the abuse.

"Hi, Chris." She raced past the stairs into the back hallway and slammed the bathroom door.

The screen door opened again and Chris's haggard-looking friend stepped inside.

"Sorry about that." Dillon waved toward the bathroom. "Ashley was desperate. She had me doing ninety on the interstate."

Chris clapped him on the back. "How's the pregnancy going?"

Dillon let out a shaky breath and raked his hand through his disheveled hair. "I'm not sure I can survive two more months of this."

A toilet flushed. Water ran in the sink. And soon the sound of bare feet slip-slapping on the wooden floor had both of them turning to see Dillon's wife heading toward them. Her sandals dangled from one hand as she stopped beside Chris.

"Sorry about the bare feet. They're so swollen the shoes were cutting off my circulation." She motioned toward Dillon. "Let me guess. He's complaining about all the suffering he's going through, right? He keeps forgetting that I'm the one birthing a watermelon." The smile on her face softened her words as she yanked on Chris's shirt so he'd lean down. She planted a kiss on his cheek and squeezed his hand. "Don't worry. I'm taking good care of him."

He raised a brow. "Him? You're having a boy?"

"No, silly. I mean, yes, we might be. Or it might be a girl. We're waiting until the birth to be surprised about the gender. I meant Dillon. I'll make sure he survives fatherhood."

Dillon plopped down in one of the recliners facing the big-screen TV mounted on the far wall. "It's not fatherhood that I'm worried about. It's the pregnancy, and childbirth." He placed a hand on his flat stomach. "Every time she throws up, I throw up. Last week, I swear I had a contraction."

Ashley clucked her tongue as she perched on the arm of his chair. "Sympathy pains." She grinned up at Chris. "Isn't it wonderful?"

Chris burst out laughing.

Dillon shot him a glare that should have set his hair on fire.

"Did you remember to bring the steaks?" Chris headed toward the abused screen door, assuming the food was in the Jeep.

"The chief has them," Dillon said. "I didn't feel well enough to go to the store so I called him to do it, instead." He pressed his hand to his stomach again and groaned as his head fell back against the chair.

Ashley rolled her eyes and plopped down onto his lap. In spite of how green Dillon looked, he immediately hugged her close and pressed a kiss on the top of her head. Dillon started to gently massage his wife's shoulders and she kissed the side of his neck. Chris had never seen two people more in love or more meant for each other. Then again, they'd only been married for close to a year. They were still newlyweds.

"Where do you want all of this stuff?" someone called from outside.

Chris turned away from the two lovebirds and looked through the screen door.

"Those two are enough to make you sick, aren't they?" fellow SWAT officer and detective Max Remington, holding a large cooler, teased from the porch.

"Hey, Max." Ashley waved over Dillon's shoulder.

"Hey, Ash." Max dipped his head toward the cooler and glanced at Chris. "This beer and ice ain't getting any lighter. Where do you want it?"

"Around back, on the deck, well away from the grill. It's hot and ready."

Max carried the cooler back down the steps. Twenty minutes later, Destiny PD's entire five-man-and-one-woman SWAT team was on the large back deck, plus Chief William Thornton, his wife, Claire, Ashley, their 911 operator—Nancy—and a handful of other support staff.

Steaks sizzled on the double-decker grill, which was Max's domain. On one side of him, SWAT officers Colby Vale and Randy Carter chatted about the best places to fish. On Max's other side a young female police intern helped load foil-wrapped potatoes and corncobs onto another section of the grill.

"Two weeks." Dillon grabbed a beer from the cooler at Chris's feet.

Since Dillon was watching Ashley talk to SWAT Officer Donna Waters a few feet away, Chris wasn't sure what he meant. "Two weeks until what?"

Dillon used his bottle to indicate the pretty young intern who was earning college credits for helping out at the Destiny police department over the summer.

"I give her and Max's fledgling relationship two more weeks, at the most," Dillon said. "They have absolutely nothing in common and she's young enough to be his…niece…or something."

Chris shrugged and snagged himself a beer from the cooler. The rest of the team laughed and talked in small groups on the massive deck. The chief and his wife were the only ones not smiling. They were too intent on discussing the best placement of the desserts on the table at the far end. Chris grinned, always amused to see the soft side of his crotchety boss whenever his wife of forty-plus years was around. He hoped someday that he'd be lucky enough to be married that long, and be just as happy. But so far he hadn't met the right woman. Given Destiny's small size, he just might have to move to another town to expand the dating pool.

The sound of an engine turning over had him stepping closer to the railing. The moving truck headed down the driveway next door, then continued up the road. His new neighbor stood in the grass beside her front porch, watching it go. Unless she was deaf, she had to hear the noise in his backyard. Was she going to ignore *all* of them?

He waited, watching. As if feeling the force of his gaze upon her, she turned. Their eyes locked and held. Then she whirled around and raced up her porch steps, the screen door slamming as she hurried inside.

"What's her name?"

Chris didn't turn at the sound of Dillon's voice. His friend braced his hands on the railing beside him.

"I have no idea," Chris answered. "She's been

here two days and she hasn't even acknowledged that I exist."

Dillon whistled low. "That's a first for you. Must be losing your touch."

He slanted his friend a look. "Yeah, well. At least I'm not puking my guts up every time someone says fried gizzards."

Dillon's eyes widened and his face went pale. A second later he clapped his hand over his mouth and ran inside the house.

Judging from the way Ashley was suddenly glaring at Chris, she'd obviously noticed Dillon's rapid retreat. She put her hands on her hips. "What did you do?"

"I might have mentioned 'fried gizzards.'"

She threw her hands in the air and shook her head in exasperation. Then she ran inside after her husband.

Chris winced at the accusatory looks some of the others gave him. He shouldn't have done that. He knew that Dillon's sympathy morning sickness could be triggered by certain foods, or even the mention of them. But teasing Dillon was just too easy—and way too fun—to resist.

He supposed he'd have to apologize later.

But right now there was something else bothering him, a puzzle he was trying to work through. He turned back toward his mysterious new neighbor's house, trying to fit the pieces together in his mind. There'd been something about her that was bothering him, the way she'd twisted her hands together as she'd stared down the road, the look in her eyes when she'd met his gaze.

And then it clicked.

He knew exactly what he'd seen.

Fear.

Chapter Three

Judging by the empty beer bottles and bags of trash sitting on his deck, Chris reckoned the annual summer-opening bash for his SWAT unit had been a success. Everyone had seemed to have a good time, even Dillon, once he'd gotten over being mad. They'd probably still be partying if the mosquitoes and gnats hadn't invaded after the sun went down.

He probably should have invited everyone to go indoors. But he'd been too preoccupied to even think of that earlier. He'd spent most of the cookout worrying about a woman he'd never met, who'd made it crystal clear that she wanted nothing to do with him.

After another glance at the house next door, he cursed and forced himself to look away. He grabbed two bags of trash in one hand and a bag of recyclables in the other. Then he headed down the deck steps and around the side yard toward the garage. He slowed as he neared the front. Behind the dark blue BMW next door was a silver Ford Taurus that hadn't been there earlier.

He shook his head. It was none of his business who the woman next door invited over. Judging by the plates on the Taurus, it was from out of town. Maybe some of her friends were helping her unpack and set up the place. Again, none of his concern.

Rounding to the front of his house, he keyed a code into the electronic keypad to open the garage door. After stowing the trash and recyclables in the appropriate bins, he closed the door again and took the front porch steps two at a time. If he hurried, he just might catch the start of a baseball game on TV.

A few minutes later, he was sitting in his favorite recliner with a beer and a bowl of popcorn on the side table. He was looking forward to a relaxing few hours vegging out before going to bed early, even though it was Saturday.

Come dawn, he had a date with a tractor and a Bush Hog and over an acre of brush to clear for Cooper, a neighbor laid up in the hospital. After that, he had his own chores to see to, including repairing some fencing to keep cows from wandering into his yard again from the farm behind his house. Sunday definitely wasn't going to be a day of rest for him. And he'd still have to catch the Sunday evening service at First Baptist or his mom would hear about it and start praying for his soul.

A piercing shriek sounded from outside, then abruptly cut off. Chris jumped up from his chair, grabbed his pistol from the coffee table. Standing stock-still, he listened for the sound again. Had a screech owl flown over the house? Maybe one of the baseball fans on TV had made the noise. Maybe. But he didn't think so. The volume on the television hadn't been turned up very loud. He pressed the mute button on the remote. Still nothing. Everything was silent. So what had he heard?

As if pulled by an unseen force, his gaze went to the window on the east side of the great room. The front of his home was about ten feet closer to the road than his neighbor's. He had a clear view of her porch, dimly lit by a single yellow bulb now that the sun had gone down. Everything looked as it had earlier when he'd dealt with the trash. Two cars were still parked in her driveway. There was no sign of any people anywhere. But he couldn't shake the uneasy feeling in his gut and the memory of the fear he'd seen in her eyes.

Cursing himself for a fool, he headed toward the screen door, gun in hand. His neighbor was probably going to think he was an idiot for checking on her. But he had to see for himself that she was okay. He shoved the pistol into his waistband at the small of his back. No sense in scaring her with his gun out. After jogging down the porch steps, he strode across the lawn to her house.

The sound of breaking glass made him pause before he reached the bottom step. An angry male voice sounded from inside. Chris whirled around, changing direction. He went to the side of the porch, where he wouldn't be visible from the front door, then hauled himself up and over the railing. Crouching down, he edged to the first window, then peeked inside.

The layout of the house was basically a one-story version of his own. He'd been in it dozens of times helping out old man Hutchinson before his family moved him to an assisted-living facility. The front door opened into the great room. The kitchen was to the left, through an archway. Both homes had a hallway that ran across the back, with two bedrooms and a bath. The only true difference was the size and the fact that Chris's home had a staircase hugging the wall on the right.

Boxes were stacked neatly across the left end of his neighbor's great room. A couch and two chairs sat in a grouping on the right. Standing in the middle of the room was a tall, lean man, his face a mask of anger as he said something to the woman across from him. Pieces of a broken drinking glass scattered the floor. But what captured Chris's attention the most was what the man was holding in his right hand—a butcher knife.

Chris ducked down, his hand going to the gun shoved into his waistband. No. He couldn't bust in there pointing his gun. The other man was too close to the woman and might hurt her. What he needed was a distraction, some way to put more distance between the two.

He also needed backup, in case this all went horribly wrong. He didn't want the woman left facing the man with the knife all by herself. He had to make sure she'd get the help she needed, no matter what.

After silencing his phone, he typed a quick text to dispatch, letting them know the situation. As expected, the immediate response was to stand down and wait for more units. Yeah, well, more units were a good thirty minutes away, best case. That was part of the price of living in the country. Like it or not, he had to go inside the house. If he waited, his neighbor could get hurt or killed by the time his fellow SWAT team members arrived.

He shoved the phone into his pocket, then hopped over the railing and dropped down to the grass. His hastily concocted plan wasn't much of a plan. It basically involved making enough noise to alert the two inside that he was there, and then going all hillbilly on them. If they were typical city slickers, as the BMW and out-of-town plates on the Taurus suggested, they might take the bait and think he was a redneck without a clue. If his gamble paid off, he'd manage to insert himself between the two and wrestle the knife away—hopefully without getting himself or anyone else killed.

Yeah, not much of a plan, but, since he couldn't think of another one, he went with it.

He wiped his palms on his jeans, then loudly clomped his booted foot onto the bottom porch step.

Chapter Four

A hollow sound echoed outside. Julie jerked around to see the sexy guy from next door stomping up the front porch steps.

"Who is that?" Alan snarled, closing the distance between them.

She swallowed, watching the knife in his hand. "My neighbor. I don't know his name."

"Get rid of him."

He edged halfway behind her, his left hand—the one holding the knife—hidden from view. Its sharp tip pressed lightly between her shoulder blades, just piercing her skin. She gasped and arched away, but the threat was still there. Her only chance was to try to appease him. If she didn't, he'd kill her, and try to kill a stranger whose only crime was that he lived next door.

A knock sounded. The tall, broad-shouldered man who'd given her so many unreturned smiles and friendly waves peered through the screen door, grinning when he saw her standing in the middle of the great room.

"Hello, there," he drawled. "I'm Chris Downing, from the house next door. Hope you don't mind me coming over. I figured it was high time I introduced myself."

"Um, actually, I don't—"

He pushed the door open and stepped inside, his white teeth gleaming in a smile that would have been charming if she wasn't so scared.

She shot a pleading look over her shoulder, then glanced back at her neighbor. "Mr. Downing, this really isn't a good—"

"Chris," he corrected, striding toward her. "No point in formalities between neighbors."

The knife pressed against her spine, a warning that she needed to do something. Fast.

"You sure are pretty, ma'am." His grin widened. "Welcome to the neighborhood." He took one of her hands in his. "And what lovely name did your mama gift you with?" He waited expectantly, his green eyes capturing hers, looking oddly serious in spite of his silly grin.

She could almost taste Alan's simmering anger, his impatience.

"I'm...ah...Julie. Julie Webb. I'm sorry but you *really* need to—"

"Can't remember the last time I met a Julie. Beautiful name for a beautiful woman." His head bobbed up and down while he vigorously shook her hand, pulling her off balance. She was forced to step toward him to keep from falling over.

Alan made a menacing sound in his throat and plopped his right hand on her shoulder, anchoring her and keeping her from moving farther away from him. But her neighbor misinterpreted the gesture. He let go of Julie's hand and offered his hand to Alan, instead.

"Didn't mean to ignore you back there," he said. "Where are my manners? Are you my new neighbor, too, or just visiting?"

The pressure on her shoulder tightened painfully, making her wince. She tensed, fully expecting to feel the bite of the knife sliding between her ribs at any moment. Most people would have read the tension between her and Alan and realized they were intruding. But her neighbor seemed oblivious, his hand still in the air, waiting for Alan to take it.

She could have sworn Alan said "stupid redneck" beneath his breath before he released her shoulder and reached around her to shake the other man's hand.

As soon as Chris's much larger hand closed around Alan's, he gave a mighty, sideways yank, ripping Alan away from Julie. Alan roared with rage and slashed at Chris with the knife. Chris twisted sideways, the blade narrowly missing his stomach. He grabbed Alan's left wrist, both men twisting and grunting with their hands joined crosswise in front of them.

"Get back," Chris yelled at Julie, twisting sideways again.

She jumped out of the way, pressing her hand

against her throat. The two men grappled like a couple of grizzly bears. Alan was shorter, but both men rippled with muscles, their biceps bulging as they strained against each other. Chris's extra height seemed to be a handicap, though. He was bent over at an impossible angle. And his hold on Alan's knife hand appeared to be slipping.

"Julie, run!"

Chris yanked Alan again. Alan countered by ducking down, trying to pull Chris off balance.

Julie couldn't seem to make her feet move. She was frozen, her throat so tight no sound would come out.

"I'm a cop," Chris bit out as he and Alan jerked and shoved at each other. "Drop the knife and we can work this out. No one needs to get hurt."

"Work it out?" Alan spit between clenched teeth. "You're the intruder. I can kill you and no one will even question me."

Chris risked a quick glance at Julie. "*Go*. Get out of here!"

She stepped back, ready to do what he'd said. But then she stopped. The room seemed to shimmer in front of her, and she was back in her bedroom five months ago. All she could see was blood, its coppery scent filling the air. It was everywhere. The floors were slippery with it. Her hands, sticky.

No. Don't think about the past. Stay in the present.

She blinked and brought the room back into focus.

"Please." She stepped forward. "Please." Another

step. She stared at Alan, willing him to look at her. "Don't do this."

Something in her voice must have captured Alan's attention. His head swiveled toward her. Bloodlust shone in his eyes. Julie knew the exact moment when he took the bait.

He gave Chris a mighty shove backward, catching him off guard. Chris stumbled, his hold on Alan broken. Julie tried to scramble back, but Alan was already lunging at her with the knife. She brought her arms up and turned her head, bracing herself.

Boom! Boom! Boom!

Alan dropped to the floor, inches away from her, unmoving. She stared at him in shock, not quite sure what had happened. Then blood began running in rivulets across the worn, uneven floor, reaching out from beneath his body like accusing fingers, pointing at her. She stumbled backward, a sob catching in her throat.

A piercing scream echoed through the room. And suddenly she was clasped tightly against Chris's chest, his arms wrapped protectively around her. He turned, blocking her view of the body lying on the floor. The screaming stopped, and she was mortified to realize that she was the one who'd been screaming.

"It's okay." One of his hands gently rubbed her back as the other cradled her against him. "He can't hurt you now."

He can't hurt me now. He can't hurt me now. She drew in a shaky breath.

Sirens wailed in the distance. How could there be sirens? She hadn't called anyone, never had a chance to call when Alan had burst into the house. But her neighbor had come inside. Chris? And he'd...shot... Alan? Yes. Those had been gunshots she'd heard. She shivered again.

"The police are on their way," he continued, speaking in a low, soothing tone. "I called them when I saw him through the window holding the knife."

The police. He'd seen Alan threatening her. Wait, wasn't *he* the police?

"I don't... I don't understand," she whispered. "What happened? Who are you?"

He gently pushed her back, his hands holding her upper arms. "I'm Christopher Downing, a detective and SWAT officer from the Destiny Police Department. I called for backup before I came in here." He scanned her from head to toe, as if searching for injuries. "Are you okay? Did he cut you?"

She blinked, her jumbled thoughts starting to come together again. "N-no. I mean, yes, he did. My back. But it's not—"

He carefully turned her around.

His fingers touched her cuts through her shirt, making them sting. She sucked in a breath.

"Sorry." He turned her to face him again. "There isn't much blood. You probably won't need stitches. Did he hurt you, in any other way?"

She frowned, trying to understand what he meant.

Then she got it. He was asking whether she'd been sexually assaulted. Heat crept up her neck.

"No, he didn't...ah...do...anything else." She pulled away, rubbing her hands up and down her arms.

The sirens had stopped. Red-and-blue lights flashed through the front windows. She was vaguely aware of a door opening, footsteps echoing on the hardwood. Chris guided her to the couch and she sat down, her gaze automatically going to the body on the floor. Deep voices spoke in quiet tones. Another voice, a woman's, said something in reply.

Blood. There was so much blood. How could one person bleed that much?

She wrapped her arms around her middle.

The couch dipped beside her. A policewoman. She was dressed in black body armor. Bright white letters across the front of her vest read SWAT.

"Hello, Ms. Webb." The woman's voice was kind, gentle. "I'm Officer Donna Waters." She waved her hands at her uniform, the gun strapped at her waist. "Don't let this gear bother you. We came prepared for a possible hostage situation." She patted Julie's hand. "An ambulance is on the way to take you to the hospital to get checked out. But you're safe now. You're going to be okay."

The woman's words seeped slowly into her brain as if through a thick fog. "Hospital? No. No, no, no. I'm not hurt. I don't want to go to a hospital."

"Ms. Webb?"

The now-familiar masculine voice had her turning her head. Chris Downing, the man who'd risked his own life for her, knelt on the floor, his expression full of compassion and concern.

"We'll take your statement after you've seen a doctor. Is there anyone I can call—"

"Is he dead?"

Her question seemed to startle him, but he quickly smoothed out his expression. "I'm afraid so, yes. Do you want me to—"

She grabbed his hands in hers and stared into his eyes. Could she trust him? Would he tell her the truth?

He frowned. "Ms. Webb—"

"Are you sure? Are you absolutely positive that he's dead?"

He had to think she was crazy. But she'd been here before. She'd been the woman sitting on the couch while the policeman told her that he was dead. And then he...wasn't. And then...and then. She shuddered.

"Is he dead?" She held her breath, waiting for his reply.

He exchanged a look with the female officer before answering. "Yes. I'm sorry. Yes, he's dead."

She covered her mouth with her hands, desperately trying to keep from falling apart.

He's dead. Oh, my God. He's dead.

"Someone will take your official statement after you've been checked out at the hospital. But can you

tell us anything right now about the man who attacked you? Did you know him?"

"Know him?" A bubble of hysterical laughter
burst between her lips. "I married him."

Chapter Five

Chris exchanged a startled look with Donna as he knelt in front of the couch. His neighbor, Julie Webb, had just announced that the intruder Chris had killed was her husband. And, instead of being angry or crying or…something that made sense, she was rocking back and forth with her arms around her middle, eyes squeezed tightly shut. The rocking wasn't the part that was odd. What had the hairs standing up on his neck were the words that she kept whispering over and over in response to him telling her that her husband was dead.

"Thank you, Lord. Thank you, thank you, thank you."

Her callous words didn't seem to match the fragile, lost look in her deep blue eyes, as if she were caught in a nightmare and couldn't find her way out. He instinctively wanted to reach for her, pull her into his arms, tell her that everything would be okay. But the words she kept chanting sent a chill up his spine and started alarm bells going off in his suspicious detective's brain.

If she'd been abused by her husband, which seemed likely given that he'd held a knife on her, Chris could understand her relief that her husband couldn't hurt her anymore. And he'd seen the fear in her eyes earlier today, which lent more evidence to the abuse theory. But he'd also seen many domestic violence cases, and almost without fail, the abused party would defend her abuser. If a cop tried to arrest the husband, or hurt him while trying to protect the wife, nine times out of ten that wife would immediately leap to the husband's defense. Julie's actions were nothing like what he was used to seeing in those cases. The whole situation just seemed…off.

"The chief's motioning for you." Donna kept her voice low. "Go on. I'll sit with her until the ambulance arrives."

He hesitated, feeling guilty for wanting to jump at her offer. He'd created this mess. He should have to stay and deal with the fallout, including whatever was going on with Julie Webb.

"It's okay. I've got this," she reassured him. "Go." She put her hand on Julie's back, lightly patting it like she would a child. Julie didn't even seem to notice. She just kept rocking and repeating her obscene prayer.

As if drawn by some invisible force, Chris's gaze slid to the body of the man who was dead because of him. This wasn't the first time he'd killed someone in the line of duty. Being on the only SWAT team within a hundred miles of Destiny meant he was often called out to help other small towns or unincorporated areas when violence landed on their doorstep. But every time he'd had to use lethal force, the what-ifs and second-guessing haunted him for a long time afterward. He didn't expect this one would be any different.

He wished he could put a sheet over the man, afford him some kind of dignity in death. But the uniformed officer standing near the body was his reminder that the scene had to be preserved until the Blount County coroner arrived. And since Destiny shared their coroner with a handful of other rural counties, that could be a while from now. Two more uniformed officers stood near a stack of boxes on the left side of the room, probably to keep Julie and others from contaminating the scene.

"Downing."

Chief Thornton's gruff voice had Chris finally standing and turning around. His boss stood just inside the front door, still wearing the khaki shorts and polo shirt that he'd worn to the cookout a few hours earlier.

"Powwow, front lawn. Now." The chief headed outside.

Chris followed the chief down the porch steps to where three members of the SWAT team who'd also been at the cookout stood waiting. Max, Randy and Colby were dressed in full body armor just like

Donna, back inside the house. It occurred to him that they must have raced like a mama sow protecting her piglets to have gotten here so fast. None of them lived close by, except for Dillon, and he was noticeably absent.

"Is Ashley okay?" he asked no one in particular, assuming the worst. He couldn't imagine his best friend not responding to a call for aid from Chris or any of their fellow officers unless something had happened to Ashley.

"She's at Blount Memorial in Maryville." Max held up his hands to stop the anticipated flood of questions. "When your 911 call came in, Dillon and Ashley were halfway to the hospital because she'd started having contractions. I assured him we could handle—"

"It's too soon," Chris interrupted, worry making his voice thick. "She's only seven months along."

"I know that," Max said. "Like I was saying, I told Dillon not to worry about you, that we had your back. And, before you ask, I spoke to him a few minutes ago. They were able to stop her labor, but they'll keep her there for observation overnight, maybe even a few days. But she and the baby are both fine."

Chris nodded, blowing out a relieved breath.

"You okay?" Max put his hand on Chris's shoulder. "You look greener than Dillon did when you mentioned fried gizzards."

"I killed a man. No. I'm not okay."

Max winced and dropped his hand, immediately making Chris regret his curt reply.

"Tell us what happened," the chief said, impatience etched on his features. "Take it from the top and don't leave anything out."

Chris began reciting the events that had led to the shooting, being as detailed as he could. Since everyone on the SWAT team performed dual roles as detectives in the fifteen-officer police force, they all listened intently, taking notes on their phones or the little pads of paper most of them kept handy.

Dillon was normally lead detective, with Chris as backup. But obviously Chris couldn't investigate a case where he was a primary participant. He wasn't sure who would run with this one.

After Chris finished his statement, the chief motioned to Max.

Max pulled a brown paper evidence bag from his rear pocket and awkwardly cleared his throat as he held it open. "Sorry, man. Standard operating procedure. Gotta take your sidearm as evidence."

Chris knew the drill and had been vaguely surprised that no one had taken his gun the moment they'd arrived. But even after putting his pistol in the bag, the weight of his now-empty holster seemed heavier than before, a reminder of what he'd done, the life he'd taken.

Max closed the bag and stepped back beside Randy. Since Max looked miserable about taking the gun, Chris gave him a reassuring nod to let him know that he understood.

"You said they were arguing when you approached the house," the chief said. "Did you hear what they were arguing about?"

He replayed the moment when he was crouching by the window, trying to remember what he'd heard.

"Seems like they both said something about 'keys,' or maybe it was 'please.' I definitely heard the man mention a gun. But he was holding a knife, so that doesn't seem right." He shrugged. "I was too far away to hear them clearly. I was more focused on what he was doing with the butcher knife and how to get it away from him."

The low wail of a siren filled the air as an ambulance turned down the road and headed toward them.

"About time," the chief said. "I was thinking we'd have to wake up Doc Brookes if it took any longer."

Chris couldn't help smiling. Even though it was only a few hours past sundown, it was probably Doc Brookes's bedtime. The town's only doctor was getting up there in years. And he made sure everyone knew not to bother him after hours unless there was arterial bleeding involved or a bone sticking out. Unfortunately, with the only hospital nearly forty-five minutes from Destiny, ornery Brookes was who they were stuck with most of the time.

"I'd better move my truck," Max said.

"Ah, shoot," Colby said. His truck's front bumper was partly blocking the end of the driveway. "Me, too."

They hurried to their vehicles to make room before the ambulance reached the house.

"Chief, got a second?" Chris asked.

Thornton looked pointedly at Randy, who took the unsubtle hint and awkwardly pounded Chris on the back before heading toward the house.

As soon as Randy was out of earshot, the chief held up his hand to stop Chris from saying anything.

"I know we still have to process the scene, and get the coroner out here, perform due diligence and all that. But honestly, son, it looks like a clean shoot to me. I can tell it's eating you up inside, but you need to let that go. You saved a life tonight. That's what you should focus on."

They moved farther into the grass while the ambulance pulled into the driveway. The EMTs hopped out of the vehicle and grabbed their gear.

"I appreciate that, Chief," Chris said. "I feel like hell for taking a life. But I know I did what I had to do. That's not what I wanted to talk to you about."

Colby and Max jogged up the driveway, having parked their trucks farther down the road. They started toward Chris and the chief, but a stern look from Thornton had them heading toward the house, instead, and following the EMTs inside.

Still, Chris hesitated. Putting his concerns into words was proving harder than he'd expected.

"Well, go on, son. Spit out whatever's bothering you. The skeeters are eatin' me alive out here."

As if to demonstrate what he'd said, the chief smacked his arm, leaving a red smear where a mosquito had been making a buffet out of him. He wiped his arm on his shorts, grimacing at the stain he'd left behind, before giving Chris an impatient look. "Well?"

"It's Mrs. Webb," Chris said. "The thing is, after the shooting, she asked me whether the guy I'd shot was dead. No, what she asked was whether I was *sure*, as if she thought I was playing a cruel joke on her, as if she *wanted* him to be dead. The guy is, *was*, her husband. And it seemed like she was...relieved...that I'd killed him."

"Well, he did hold a knife on her. Makes sense she'd be happy to be alive and that she didn't have to worry about him attacking her again."

Chris scrubbed his face and then looked down the dark road, lit only by the occasional firefly. Crickets and bullfrogs competed with one another in their nightly symphony. All in all, everything seemed so normal. And, yet, nothing was the same.

"You think there's more to it than that, don't you?" The chief was studying him intently. "Why?"

"Because she didn't ask me just once whether he was dead. She asked several times. And it was more the way she asked it that spooked me. You know how it is. If there's a domestic dispute, a husband beating his wife or trying to kill her, we cops intervene and suddenly we're the bad guys. Happens almost every time. But I shoot Mrs. Webb's husband and she starts praying out loud, thanking God. I don't know about you, but that's a first for me."

Thornton was quiet for a long moment, leaving Chris to wallow in his own thoughts, to wonder if saying anything was the right thing to do. He hated the unflattering picture that he'd just painted of Julie Webb. It didn't seem right, as if he was spreading rumors, gossiping—something his father would have rewarded with an extra long switch applied liberally to his hide. But this wasn't high school. This was the real world, a death investigation, where actions and words had consequences. They mattered. And he couldn't ignore something just because it was uncomfortable.

"How did she seem before all of this?" Thornton finally asked. "If her husband had a history of violence against her, she might have joined a support group and got the help she needed to cut all ties. Maybe she moved here to escape him, thought she was safe. But he figured out where she was, came after her. Seems to me that'd make her mighty grateful that he's never going to hurt her again."

"Maybe." He wanted to believe that was it. But even he could hear the doubt in his voice. He shrugged. "Hard to say what her state of mind was prior to this incident. She kept to herself, didn't even wave. I did get the feeling earlier today, when I saw her on her porch, that she was afraid of…something. And that was before her husband showed up."

"There, see? It's like I said. Her behavior could very well make sense, given those circumstances. And she's lucky you were close by to save her."

"Yeah," he mumbled. "Lucky for both of us."

The chief gave him a knowing look. And it dawned on Chris that Thornton might know first-hand how he felt. Chris had joined the force right out of college, thirteen years ago. But Thornton was already chief by then. There was no telling what horrors he might have faced as a young beat cop, or even in his detective days, what burdens he might have accumulated like an invisible weight that no one else could see. All Chris knew for sure was what *he* felt, which was all kinds of uneasy about this whole thing.

It was bad enough that he'd taken a life. Even worse if there was something else going on here. The "something else" that kept running through his mind was so prejudicial against Julie Webb that he couldn't voice it to the chief, not without proof, something concrete. All he had was a disturbing series of impressions that had begun to take root in his mind from the moment he'd seen her reaction to the shooting.

Suspicions that maybe this wasn't "just" a case of a domestic dispute with tragic consequences.

That maybe Julie Webb knew she was moving in next door to a cop all along.

That she had planned this whole thing from beginning to end.

That she'd just used Chris as a weapon to commit murder.

Chapter Six

Standing in the Destiny Police Department at midnight on a Saturday wasn't exactly where Chris imagined his fellow SWAT team members wanted to be. But not one of them had even considered going home. Max, Colby, Donna and Randy stood shoulder to shoulder with him in a show of solidarity while they watched their boss interview Julie Webb through the large two-way glass window.

Behind Chris and his SWAT team, two more officers sat at desks on the other side of the large open room that was essentially the entire police station. One of them, Blake Sullivan, was a recent transfer and would eventually be a detective and member of their SWAT team. But not yet. For now, he was learning the ropes of Destiny PD as a nightshift cop, which included filling out a lot of mundane reports.

There were fifteen desks in all, three rows of five. And other than a couple of holding cells off the back wall and a bathroom, there was just the chief's office, his executive washroom that the team loved to tease him about and the interview room.

The entire night shift consisted of the two officers currently writing reports and two more out on patrol. Destiny wasn't exactly a mecca for crime. The town didn't boast a strip of bars or clubs to spill their drugs or drunks into the streets. A typical night might mean lecturing some teenagers caught drag racing, or rescuing a rival football team's stolen mascot from a hayloft.

Tonight was anything but typical.

Tonight a man had died.

And Chris wanted, *needed*, to find out what had precipitated the violence by Alan Webb, leaving Chris no choice but to use lethal force. The chief had officially placed him on administrative leave, pending the results of the investigation. He'd expressly forbidden Chris from going into the interview room. But since the chief would've had to fight his own SWAT team to force Chris to leave the station, he'd wisely pretended not to notice him in the squad room, watching the chief interview the witness.

Along with her counsel, assistant district attorney Kathy Nelson.

Plus two administrative lackeys—Brian Henson and Jonathan Bolton—that Nelson had brought with her from Nashville. She'd left the two men sitting at one of the desks on the opposite side of the squad room like eager lapdogs waiting for their master to give them an order.

Chris studied Henson and Bolton for a long moment before looking back at the interview window. "If she felt she needed a lawyer, why call an ADA? And since when does an assistant district attorney have an entourage? Or drive with that entourage for three hours in the middle of the night for a witness interview, let alone one that's way outside her jurisdiction?"

"Right? Doesn't make a lick of sense," Donna said beside him.

After dodging another barrage of questions like the polished politician that she was, Nelson shoved back her chair and stood.

"Wait, what's she doing?" Max asked.

Nelson motioned to Mrs. Webb. She picked up her purse from the table and stood.

Chris stiffened. "They're leaving."

Donna was clearly bemused. "But they didn't answer hardly any of the chief's questions."

"Screw this." Chris stepped toward the interview room door.

Max grabbed his shoulder. "Don't do it, man. The chief will—"

Chris shoved Max's hand away and yanked open the door.

JULIE HURRIEDLY STEPPED back to put more distance between her and the imposing man suddenly filling the open doorway of the interview room—her neighbor, Detective Chris Downing. With his clenched jaw and hands fisted at his sides, he seemed like a tautly drawn bow, ready to spring.

Before Kathy could say anything, Thornton held his hand out to stop her and confronted his officer.

"I warned you, Chris. You can't be in here." His gravelly voice whipped through the room. "What do I have to do, arrest you? Lock you in a cell?"

Twin spots of color darkened Chris's cheekbones. His heated gaze flashed to Julie, then back to Thornton. "I need answers. And, so far, you're not getting any. Let me interview her. I'll make her talk."

Julie flinched at his harsh tone. She'd retreated to her chair, but even with a table between them, his anger seemed to fill the room, crowding in on her. Where was the gentle, concerned man who'd knelt in front of the couch earlier this evening, reassuring her that everything was going to be okay?

Kathy didn't move. Her only concession to Chris standing so close was to tilt her head back to meet his gaze. "Are you threatening Mrs. Webb, Officer Downing?"

Thornton aimed an aggravated look at Kathy. "It's *Detective*, not *Officer*. And he's not threatening anyone. Stay out of this."

The shocked look on Kathy's face was almost comical. Julie doubted that anyone, except maybe Kathy's husband, had ever dared to speak to her that way before. She seemed to be at a loss as to how to respond.

"Don't you be questioning my methods, son."

Thornton jabbed his finger at Chris's chest. "I was interviewing witnesses when you were knee-high to a mule. Since you're the one who fired the gun, you can't be involved in the investigation. Until this is over, you're a civilian. And civilians have no business questioning witnesses. Now, turn around and—"

"No." Julie jumped up from her seat.

Everyone stared at her in surprise.

She cleared her throat, just as surprised as they were at her outburst, but she now acknowledged what her subconscious had already known—that this was the right thing to do.

"I want him to stay," she said.

The expression on Chris's face turned suspicious.

"What did you say?" Thornton's question sounded more like he was daring her to repeat her request, a request he had no intention of fulfilling.

"Julie—" Kathy began.

She waved her hand. "Taking a life is a heavy burden that no one should have to bear, even if taking that life was necessary. Letting Detective Downing ask questions about why he was put in that situation is the least that I can do to show my gratitude for his saving my life. So, Chief Thornton, either you allow him to stay, or the interview is over."

While Thornton stood in indecision, Chris firmly closed the door and then straddled the chair directly across from her. He gave her a crisp nod, as if to grudgingly thank her. She nodded in return, just as stiffly—two adversaries facing off before a fight.

The other two gave up their vigil. Kathy sat down while Thornton stared pointedly at his chair, the one Chris was currently occupying. Chris ignored him. After grumbling something beneath his breath about "seat stealers," the chief finally sat down. But the table's small size and Chris's broad shoulders had forced the chief to the end of the table, which had him grumbling again.

Julie waited expectantly. Rather than attack her with a volley of questions, Chris simply stared at her, as if sizing her up. If he was trying to figure out how to intimidate her, the effort was unnecessary. She'd been intimidated since the moment he'd stood in the open doorway like a fierce warrior looking for a dragon to slay.

And she was the dragon.

She clasped her hands beneath the table so he couldn't see that they were shaking. It wasn't just Chris that had her so nervous. Being in an interrogation room again, after all these months, stirred up a host of horrific memories. The past few months had been rough, brutal. But at least she'd survived. Her husband hadn't. And even though she was relieved she no longer had to fear him, she still grieved that it had come to this. There'd been a time once, long ago, when she'd loved him.

He'd been a good man back then—handsome, kind, sweet, helping her move forward after the

tragic loss of her family just a few months before
she'd met him. She grieved for *that* Alan, the one
she'd pledged to honor and love until death do they
part. The man who had, or so she liked to believe,
loved her, too, once upon a time, until the fairy tale
had twisted into a tragedy.

"Mrs. Webb?" Chris's deep voice intruded into
her thoughts. "Please answer the question."

She blinked. "I'm sorry. What did you ask me?"

"I'll answer your question," Kathy interrupted.
"Mrs. Webb came to Destiny to hide from her abusive husband."

Julie shot the other woman an irritated look.
She made it sound like Julie had stayed with Alan
through a long, abusive relationship. In truth, before
today, Alan had been abusive only once, five months
ago. After that one horrific night, she'd filed for divorce and ended her three-year marriage. She supposed she was lucky. Some women ended up caught
in cycles of violence from which they could never
escape. But Julie wasn't feeling particularly fortu-
nate at the moment. Everything was in turmoil. And
Alan had lost his life. There was no way to feel good
about what had happened.

"Her husband somehow found out that she was
here, in Destiny," Kathy continued. "And he broke
into her home and assaulted her. The rest you know.
Detective Downing had to use deadly force to protect her."

"How about we let the witness give her own statement," Chris said, closely watching Julie. "Mrs. Webb—"

"Julie, please," she corrected, so tired of the awkwardness and formalities of this never-ending interview. At this point she just wanted it over.

"Julie," he corrected. "Do you agree with the assistant district attorney's version of this evening's events?"

She hesitated, then nodded.

Kathy let out a breath, as if relieved.

"Except for the part where she made it sound like my husband had a history of violence," she said. "Alan and I never had a perfect marriage. But until... recently...he never lifted a hand against me. Something...happened to make him snap." She finished in a near whisper, her defense of Alan sounding weak when she said it out loud. Still, she hated to paint him as a bad person when, for most of the time that she'd known him, he was kind and good to her.

Kathy put a hand on top of Julie's and gave her a sympathetic look. "You're being far too kind to a man who tried to kill you."

Julie swallowed and looked away.

Kathy sighed and turned in her seat to face Julie. "For the record, are you stating that your husband wasn't dangerous? That you weren't afraid of him?"

"No, of course not. He was definitely dangerous. You know what he did in Nashville."

Kathy groaned and closed her eyes.

"I was wondering why you hadn't brought that

up yet." Thornton jumped on her statement. "I ran your husband's name through the computer before the interview. Why don't you tell us your version of the first attack?"

Chris shot a surprised look at his boss. Julie figured he must not have been told what Thornton had found.

Kathy checked her watch, probably calculating how late—or early in the morning now—it would be by the time this was over and she could start the long drive back.

"You might as well tell them," she said. "Now that you've brought it up. Then I'll take you back to Nashville and—"

"I'm not going back."

Kathy frowned. "Why not?"

"I just got here. I don't want to move again. Not this soon."

"You were here to hide out from Alan. Obviously, that's not necessary anymore."

"We don't know if he was the one flattening my tires, salting my yard, and everything else. What if it was his family? I wouldn't put it past them."

"I don't think they're dangerous," Kathy said.

"We both know what they can be like," she said. "I'd much rather stay here until everything is settled. Then maybe they'll finally leave me alone and I can return home and live in peace."

Kathy shrugged. "Maybe it does make sense to stay here, at least until the civil case is over."

"Civil case?" Thornton's voice had risen again and he looked like he was ready to explode with frustration. "This is supposed to be an interview, a police interview. You two need to start talking to *us*, instead of to each other. You need to answer our questions."

"Chief—" Kathy began.

"What did he do to you?" Chris's deep voice cut through the conversation, silencing everyone in the room. His brow was furrowed with concern, his tone gentle, almost a whisper, just like back at the house. "How did he hurt you?"

Her stomach did a little flip. Part of her was tempted to throw herself in his arms and beg him to take her away from the nightmare that her life had become. She must be more exhausted than she thought. Chris had shown his true colors when he'd barged into the room, looking like a bull ready to charge after a red flag. He wasn't really interested in helping her. She'd do well to remember that, and not let her exhaustion and longing for someone to lean on after all these months of being alone influence her decisions.

She straightened her spine and focused on Thornton as she answered. If she looked at the supposed concern on Chris's face one more time she just might shatter.

"The reason I moved to Destiny was to hide from my husband, as Kathy said. He disappeared after posting bail. And there have been some…incidents, annoyances really, that made me wonder if he was stalking me. While it's true that he doesn't have a...*long* history of being abusive, he did attack me about five months ago, which you obviously already know. We were separated. He'd moved out and left the house to me. And then he broke into our home in the middle of the night. He was dressed all in black and wore a mask. And that night, like earlier today, he had a knife. Today, Detective Downing saved my life when he shot Alan. And I deeply appreciate his sacrifice. But there wasn't anyone else around months ago to protect me. So I saved myself. I grabbed my husband's gun, the one he'd left in the nightstand before moving out, and I shot him."

Chris blinked in surprise. "You shot your husband?"

"I did."

Thornton and Chris exchanged a glance. But Julie had no clue what they were silently communicating to each other.

Kathy said, "Mr. Webb was charged with breaking and entering and attempted murder. He had duct tape, a knife and gloves. He attacked Mrs. Webb, pulled her out of the bed and onto the floor. She was able to get away and grab the gun or she wouldn't be sitting here today. She'd be buried six feet under. However, in spite of the overwhelming evidence in the case, the judge went against our recommendations and set bail at one million dollars, which Mr. Webb immediately paid. Then he—"

"He paid a million-dollar bail?" Thornton asked.

He and Chris both looked at Julie with renewed interest. "Just how much money did he have? And who's the beneficiary?"

She closed her eyes and squeezed her hands together in her lap. This was what she'd wanted to avoid. Now they would look at her the way Alan's family did. They'd never believed her side of what had happened and had accused her of trying to kill him for his money.

Kathy said something to Thornton but Julie tuned it out. She just wanted the interview to be over. How had it come to this? As she often did when thinking about the past year of her life, when her marriage had started to fail, she tried to pinpoint that one decision, that one pivotal event that had led to her entire life being turned upside down. But she still didn't know what had happened. One day she was happy, *they* were happy, her and Alan. The next, everything had changed. Alan had become moody, angry, and it continued to go downhill from there. A tear ran down her cheek. Then another. She drew a shaky breath and wiped them away.

"Here." Chris was crouching beside her chair, holding a box of tissues. And in his other hand was a bottle of water, which he held out to her. "They're so busy arguing with each other over there that they didn't even notice I'd left the room to get you the water and tissues."

He jerked his head toward the corner by the window where Thornton and Kathy were standing, having a heated argument. Apparently, Julie had been so lost in her own thoughts, she hadn't noticed anything that had happened over the past few minutes, either.

She wiped her cheeks with a tissue, then took the bottle. He'd already opened it and had set the cap on the table.

"Thank you," she said.

"You're welcome." He gestured toward the corner again. "I think they're going to be at this for a while. Want to get out of here?"

She blinked. "I thought you wanted to interview me? Or is that your plan, to take me somewhere else and ask me questions without Kathy present?"

He cocked his head, looking every bit the handsome, sexy neighbor again instead of the angry, hardened cop. "Do you trust me?"

"No."

He laughed. "Score one for honesty."

"Sorry."

"Don't be. Never apologize for telling the truth." He glanced at the chief and Kathy, completely consumed in their argument, before looking at Julie again. "I'd like to remind you that I'm a police officer, sworn to protect and serve. And if that doesn't make you trust me, I'll resort to blackmail."

"Blackmail?"

His grin faded, and he was once again staring at her with an intensity that was unnerving. "Like you said before, I deserve answers. So how about we ditch this place and I take you somewhere safe, where no one will bother you? We'll both get a good night's sleep. No questions. No talking unless you want to. Then tomorrow, we take a fresh look at the situation and figure out where to go from there. Sound good?"

"Sounds too good, actually. Why are you offering?"

"Because somewhere along the way this interview turned into an inquisition. The chief and I both want answers, so I don't want Nelson convincing you to leave and never come back. But it's late, we're all tired and you aren't a criminal being interrogated. You're a witness, a victim. You deserve to be treated better than you have been. I'm offering a truce. What do you say? Will you let me get you out of here?" He stood and held out his hand.

This time it was her turn to glance at Thornton and Kathy. Both their faces were red. Whatever they were arguing about, it didn't look like they'd stop anytime soon.

She put her hand in Chris's. "Let's go."

Chapter Seven

Chris glanced at his passenger as he turned his pickup off the highway onto a gravel road. Thanks to his SWAT team, he'd managed to get the witness out of the station without Henson or Bolton being able to give chase. It was hard to follow someone when the only exit door was blocked by three cops with guns. But he was already having buyer's remorse.

The chief was going to kill him for this.

Julie sat stiffly, clutching the armrest as if it were a lifeline, staring through the windshield. Was she also regretting the decision to flee? Wondering if she'd gotten herself into worse trouble than she was already in?

"This isn't the way I go to my house." She leaned forward to peer at the narrow gravel road and trees crowding in that were revealed in the headlights. "I assumed you were taking me home. Is this a back way?"

"Your home is still taped off as a crime scene. You can't go there until it's released."

Her shoulders slumped, but she nodded. "This seems awfully far from town to be leading to a hotel."

"It's called Harmony Haven. You'll see the place over that next rise. See how the sky is lighter up ahead? That's from the security and landscape lights."

"A bed-and-breakfast then?"

He steered around a pothole, surprised the road was in such poor condition. Then again, there'd been a lot of rain this past month, and he hadn't been down this way in quite a while.

"Chris?"

He shook his head. "It's not a B and B. It's a private home on a horse-rescue farm. It belongs to my friends Dillon and Ashley. They're not here right now and I figured they wouldn't mind us crashing for the night."

Any argument she might have been about to give was forgotten as they topped the rise and Dillon's property came into view. Julie stared in wonder at the beautiful vista laid out before them. It pleased him that she seemed so awestruck. He felt that way every time he came here, especially at night because of the way the lights cast an ethereal glow on the place.

With the sweat equity he'd invested to help Dillon get this place up and running over the years, he couldn't help feeling proprietary about it. But with Dillon married now, Chris's visits had become less frequent. Newlyweds needed their privacy, even more so now with a baby on the way. His jaw tightened. If it weren't so late, he'd call the hospital for an update on Ashley. He'd have to remember to call first thing in the morning and check on her.

He pulled the truck to a stop beside the two-story white farmhouse and took a moment to enjoy the view himself. Soft floodlights that Ashley had insisted upon, which were more for ambience than security, dotted a long, pristine, white three-rail fence and acres and acres of lush green pastures that went on forever.

The enormous stable was partially visible behind the house. He parked at the end of the home's enormous wraparound front porch that boasted white rockers and an old-fashioned swing hanging from chains.

"It's beautiful," Julie whispered, seemingly mesmerized as the light breeze teased the swing back and forth, the chains creaking in rhythm with the sound of cicadas.

"I reckon it is." He cut the engine, admiring her profile. The lights from the yard sparkled on the honey-blond highlights in her brown hair. She had a small, pert nose and pale skin with a smattering of freckles across both cheeks. A lock of her hair hung forward and he barely resisted the urge to brush it back.

"Harmony Haven," she whispered, as if testing the name on her tongue. "You said it's a horse rescue?"

He waved toward the stable, the main doors sealed up for the night. "There are a couple dozen horses in there, another dozen or so out in the pasture. Ashley and Dillon run horse camps every summer and adopt out most of the herd. Then rescues trickle in throughout the year and they work on rehabilitating them, regaining their trust. A couple months from now this year's first campers will arrive. There's a bunkhouse farther out for the farmhands and a second bunkhouse for the campers."

"Ashley and Dillon are married?"

He nodded. "Almost a year now."

"Then who's Harmony?"

Chris's smiled faded. "Dillon's baby sister. She loved horses even more than he does, which seems impossible."

"Loved? Past tense?"

"She died a long time ago. Hang tight. I'll help you down."

Before she could ask him any more questions or dredge up memories of the past, he hopped down from the truck and hurried to the passenger side. Although his black four-by-four was suspended a lot higher than the average pickup, it wasn't quite a monster truck. It was just high enough for his six-foot-two frame to be comfortable climbing in and out. But Julie was almost a foot shorter than him, which meant he'd had to lift her up into the truck back at the station. Something he'd realized he didn't mind one bit. She sure was a pretty thing.

She'd just opened her door when he reached her. With a mumbled apology, he put his hands at her waist and lifted her down. As soon as her shoes touched the ground, she stepped back, forcing him to drop his hands. She seemed awkward, uncomfortable as she smoothed her blouse over her khaki pants.

"Why didn't we go to a hotel?" She followed him as he led the way toward the front porch. "Why drive so far from town?"

He stopped with his boot on the bottom step. "There's only one hotel in Destiny. Nelson would have looked for you there."

Her brows shot up. "I didn't know we were hiding from her."

He smiled. "We're hiding more from my boss than from your ADA. I'm on administrative leave, which means I'm not even supposed to talk to you."

"But you want answers, like you said at the station."

He nodded.

"You aren't too good at following orders, are you?"

"Not when I'm shut out of a case where I had to kill a man."

She swallowed and looked away.

"Look," he said. "I'm not going to force you to do anything you don't want to do. For now, we're just escaping the inquisition back there and getting a good night's sleep. As a bonus, I ensure that Nelson doesn't whisk you off to Nashville overnight."

She stood on the first step, then moved up one more, making her almost eye level with him.

"You seem to think that if Kathy tells me to do

something, I jump to do it. What gave you that impression?"

He shrugged. "I think it's more that she drove three hours to come to your rescue. Allowing you to talk anymore to us would have pretty much defeated the purpose in her driving down here. Lawyers don't want their clients to talk. Ever."

He took the stairs two at a time and paused at the door.

When she joined him there, he added, "This place has the best security around. No one is going to sneak up on you while you're here. You're safe."

Her lips parted in surprise.

He shook his head, exasperated. "Did you really think I was buying the picture that Nelson was painting? It's as obvious as the day is long that you're both hiding something, holding something back. And if you moved to Destiny just to hide from your husband, or little high school-type pranks, you wouldn't still be scared."

She stiffened. "What makes you think I'm scared?"

He glanced at her hands, which she was twisting together.

She jerked them apart, her face flushing again.

"I guess the real question is whether Nelson knows whatever secrets you're hiding."

Her expression went blank, as if she'd thrown up a wall. He'd been fishing, but now he knew for sure that she really was hiding something. What could she be hiding that even her ADA friend didn't know about? And why?

She looked at the truck as if debating whether to demand that he take her back to town. Sensing that if he pushed her on it, if he argued to get her to stay, that she'd push back and demand to leave, he remained silent and waited.

"Your friends Dillon and Ashley—they know we're here? You have keys to the house?"

In answer, he separated the keys on his key ring and held up one. "If Dillon is awake, he knows. The security system texted him our picture as soon as we turned down the private road to the farm."

Her eyes widened.

"I'm sure they don't mind," he continued. "But I'll call in the morning and explain the situation."

"Okay, then. I'll stay. Just for the night."

He unlocked the door and waved her inside before she could change her mind.

Chapter Eight

Of all the reckless, crazy things that Julie had ever done, sneaking off with Detective Chris Downing was probably the most outrageous and stupid. She couldn't believe that she'd had the gumption to tiptoe out of the conference room, pausing only briefly as he whispered to his SWAT team members, and then getting into his pickup truck.

When he'd handed her that tissue in the conference room to wipe her tears, it was as if they were co-conspirators, the two of them against the world. And she'd been just desperate enough to take the lifeline that he'd offered, tricking herself into believing that he was someone she could trust. He'd been what she'd needed most at that very moment—someone to lean on, someone who would keep her safe, be a friend, if only for one night.

She was such a fool.

They had a truce, more or less, but she knew the limits. The moment she got up tomorrow he'd probably barrage her with questions, and she wouldn't have Kathy here to deflect them. She might as well have stayed at the police station.

As she followed him inside, he paused beside a beeping security alarm keypad and keyed in the security code, disabling it. After locking the door, he set the alarm again and waved his hand to encompass the large open room.

"This is it," he said. "Dillon took down most of the walls to give it an open floor plan. As you can see, the kitchen is on the back left. Feel free to grab something if you're thirsty or hungry."

She nodded, noting the granite-topped island that separated the kitchen from the great room. A straight staircase was in front of them, with a small dark hallway opening behind it on the main floor. The room was an eclectic mix of masculine and feminine touches, with dark chunky wood furniture softened by pastel throws and pillows, and rugs scattered across the hardwood floor.

"Your room is through there." He led her through a doorway on the right, just past the front door. "This is the in-law suite, with its own private bath. Ashley's expecting her parents to stay here for a few weeks after the baby is born. So I'm sure she's already got it stocked with everything you could possibly need—shampoo, toothbrushes, stuff like that. But if there's something else you need, let me know. I can check upstairs."

"I'm sure I'll be fine." She hesitated by the four-poster bed. "I didn't even think about packing a bag when I left my house."

"We wouldn't have let you anyway."

Her gaze shot to his in question.

"Your house is a crime scene," he reminded her.

"Oh." She twisted her hands together, then remembered him noticing her doing that before when she was nervous and she forced her hands apart.

"We'll call Donna in the morning. She's one of the SWAT officers. You met her, just after…"

"I remember," she said, thinking back to the kind woman who'd sat beside her on the couch, while Alan lay on the floor not far away. She swallowed against the bile rising in her throat and rubbed her hands up and down her arms.

Looking uncomfortable, Chris shifted on his feet. "She can get you whatever you need from the house."

She nodded. "What about you? You'll need a bag, too."

He shook his head. "I stay here sometimes when Dillon and I brainstorm cases, or when we have to get an early start during hunting season. Don't stay nearly as often as I used to. But I've still got stuff in a guest room upstairs." He waved toward the doorway to the great room. "If you want, we can see if Ashley has a nightgown that will fit you. I'm sure she wouldn't mind. You two are close to the same size, although you're a bit shorter."

"I don't want to impose any more than I already have."

"You're not imposing. Trust me. Ashley and Dillon would give the shirts off their backs to someone in need."

Trust him. She wished it were that easy. But she'd given her trust before, and it had nearly killed her.

She forced a smile. "I'll be okay without borrowing any clothes. Where will you stay? The guest room you mentioned upstairs?"

His gaze dropped to her hands, and she realized she was twisting them together again. She tugged them apart and tried to keep her expression neutral. She didn't want him to know that she was already getting scared again. It was stupid, ridiculous, to be worried about anyone finding her way out here. But Alan had found her. And that meant that anyone could. So what was she going to do? Going home to Nashville didn't seem like a good option. But neither did staying here. She hadn't been thinking clearly when she'd told Kathy that she wasn't leaving. She should go somewhere else. But how could she leave without a destination in mind?

Chris was studying her. What did he see? Again, she tried to keep her expression neutral, to hide the doubts, the questions, even the fear roiling through her mind.

Finally, he said, "I like the couch down here just fine. If you need anything, just holler."

The couch. This house was huge, probably had four or five bedrooms upstairs, and he was taking the couch. Either he was an old-fashioned Southern gentleman and truly wanted to be close by if she needed him, or he suspected something and didn't want to let her out of his sight. She thought about arguing with him, to try to get him to go upstairs. But that would probably only make him suspicious, if he wasn't already.

"Thank you," she said.

He tipped his head as if he were wearing a hat, but continued to stand there.

The silence drew out between them.

She motioned toward the cell phone on his belt. "I'm surprised your boss hasn't called you by now."

"Ringer's off. What about Nelson?" He waved at her purse. "I assume you've got a cell phone in there. But she hasn't called you."

"Ringer's off."

They both smiled.

He motioned toward the clock on the bedside table. "The sun will be coming up sooner than you think. I reckon we'd better get some sleep while we can." He tipped his head again. "Good night, Julie."

"Good night...Chris."

His smile broadened, and then he stepped through the doorway. He'd just grabbed the doorknob when she called out to him.

"Chris?"

He glanced back in question.

"Tomorrow, when news of my husband's death spreads, when Kathy tells his family what happened, they'll demand justice. They'll accuse me of orchestrating his death. They'll say some really awful, terrible things about me."

His brows furrowed.

She took a step toward him, then another, until the tips of her shoes pressed against the tips of his boots. "But I promise you, I didn't plan any of this. I would never have placed you in the position that you were in today if I could have prevented it. I'm so sorry that you got involved."

He slowly raised his hand toward her, giving her every chance to step away.

She didn't.

He feathered his fingers across her cheek, pushing back some of the hair that had fallen across her face. But, instead of dropping his hand, he cupped her cheek, as he stared down into her eyes. She felt the warmth of his touch all the way to her toes.

"Who else are you afraid of?" he whispered.

She wanted to trust him, to ask for his help. But this wasn't his fight. She couldn't involve him any more than she already had.

She gently pulled his hand down, squeezed it, then let it go.

"Good night, Chris."

He hesitated, then nodded. "Good night, Julie."

The door closed behind him. She sat down on the bed, listening to the sounds of the house settling around her, to the sound of him going upstairs, probably to get sheets and pillows for the couch. Water ran in the bathroom down the hall a few minutes later. And not long after that, the light under the door went dark.

She continued to sit on the bed, thinking about what had happened, about what would happen tomorrow, about what she needed to do. She twisted her hands in her lap, watching the minutes tick by on the clock. When the clock struck two, she stood and grabbed her purse.

Chapter Nine

Chris used the tongs to put the last piece of bacon onto the paper-towel-lined plate with the others and turned off the stove. He shoved the hot pan of grease into the oven to be cleaned later once it cooled, then stepped back to make sure he hadn't forgotten anything.

Other than throwing the occasional steak or ribs on a grill when he had friends over and Max wasn't there as the master chef, cooking wasn't his thing. He tended to live on cereal, sandwiches and an occasional hot meal of catfish and grits at Mama Jo's Kitchen back in town. But since he'd practically kidnapped Julie last night, he figured paying her back with a stick-to-the-ribs breakfast was the least he could do.

Dillon's wife, Ashley, was one of the best cooks he'd ever met. Her kitchen was stocked with everything he could possibly need to prepare a feast—or, in this case, scrambled eggs with cheese, fried bacon and toast. He'd looked for canned biscuits to cook, but premade dough was probably an affront to someone like Ashley. She probably made them from scratch, which was beyond his capabilities. He'd had to settle for whole-wheat toast.

Now, all he had to do was go wake Julie. He checked his watch. Seven-thirty. On a normal day he'd have been at the office for a good hour by now. Maybe Julie wasn't an early riser like him. They had been up awfully late last night. And goodness knew she'd been through a terrible ordeal. He'd assumed the smell of bacon and freshly brewed coffee would bring her into the kitchen. But if she was too exhausted for those delicious smells to lure her out of bed, maybe he should give her just a little bit longer to sleep. Everything could be reheated. And he did have some calls to make.

He covered the food with paper towels to keep it from getting cold and plopped down at the table. The first call he made was to Dillon. After getting an update on Ashley and the baby, he explained to Dillon about what was going on with the case and why he'd crashed at Harmony Haven for the night. As expected, Dillon didn't mind one bit and had already seen the security camera text to let him know that Chris was there.

The second call didn't go nearly so well.

"What the hell were you thinking?" his boss yelled.

Chris winced and held the phone several inches from his ear. He waited until the yelling stopped before risking holding the phone closer. After suffering through a chastisement that had him feeling like a five-year-old, he explained his reasons to his boss and agreed that he'd go ahead and bring Julie to the police station after breakfast.

Nelson had left for Nashville late last night after the chief had essentially lied to smooth things over. He'd made it sound like it had been his idea all along for Chris to take Julie to some safe house for the night and that they'd escort her to Nashville today once she'd had a good night's rest. The chief said Nelson had seemed more than happy to believe him as she had a heavy caseload back in town.

Of course, Chris and the others had no intention of taking Julie to Nashville. Not until they'd gotten to the bottom of their investigation. But Nelson didn't need to know that.

He hung up and checked his watch again. The chief, of course, wanted them at the station ASAP. But with the ADA out of the picture, at least temporarily, there wasn't as much of a rush in Chris's opinion. He'd let Julie get a little more sleep, give her a hot breakfast, then they'd head back to town. Until he knew for sure just how "innocent" she was in what had happened at her house, he was going to try to give her the benefit of the doubt and treat her as a victim and a witness rather than like someone with more skin in the game. But he wasn't going to let those soft, doe eyes of hers make him let down his guard, either. Maybe he could ask her the questions he was dying to ask on the way to the station, too. This administrative leave thing was going to make it next to impossible to get answers once he turned her over to his boss.

He shoved his phone back into the holder on his belt as a knock sounded at the back kitchen door. Recognizing the silhouette of Dillon's main farmhand behind the filmy white curtain covering the glass, Chris waved in greeting. He hurried to the door and reached up to key the security code into the electronic keypad by the door. But the light wasn't red. It was green.

The alarm was already disarmed.

He yanked his backup gun out of his ankle holster, since the chief had made him turn over his primary gun, and held it down by his thigh. He had two more pistols locked in the pickup. He'd have to remember to strap one of those on his belt when he left. On duty or off, he didn't want to get caught without enough firepower if the need arose. Especially if someone was still after Julie Webb—which seemed possible based on the fear he'd still seen in her eyes last night.

He threw the door open. "Griffin, you seen anyone skulking around here?"

The answering smile on Griffin's sun-browned face was replaced with concern as he glanced around. "Just the workers, feeding the horses, mucking stalls. I saw your truck and thought you might have an update on Miss Ashley."

"Stay here."

Without waiting for the older man to reply, Chris hurried from the kitchen, through the great room to the still-closed door of the front guest room. He didn't stop to knock. He threw the door open, sweeping his pistol out in front of him, fully expecting to see an intruder standing over Julie's bed or perhaps already holding her hostage.

There wasn't anyone there. The bed didn't even look like it had been slept in.

"Chris?" Griffin had obviously ignored his order to stay put and was behind him in the doorway.

Chris ignored him and cleared the closet, then the attached bath, before turning around. He strode across the room, the gun still at his side.

"What's going on?" Griffin asked, quickly backing up to let him through the doorway. "Should I call 911?"

"Not yet." He headed to his right, beside the staircase to the back hallway and the room at the back right corner of the downstairs. He headed inside and pulled up a chair in front of the main security camera console.

"Is Miss Ashley okay? Did something happen?"

The worry in Griffin's voice as he ran into the room finally sank in and Chris turned to face him. Last year Ashley had nearly been killed by some very bad people who were after her. Griffin had probably seen Chris's gun and thought the worst.

"She's fine. She and the baby are both fine. Dillon's with them at the hospital. They were able to stop the contractions, but they're keeping her for observation for a few days."

"*Gracias a Dios*. Thank God," Griffin whispered, making the sign of the cross on his chest. "I thought the bad men were back again to hurt Miss Ashley."

A pang of guilt shot through Chris for not taking a few extra seconds at the back door to reassure the old man. From what Dillon had told him, Griffin still had nightmares about the siege that had happened here when the men had caught up to Ashley last year.

Chris flipped on the computer monitors and entered the password into the menu to access the security footage. "Like I said, Ashley and the baby are fine. I'm here for another reason entirely." He keyed in some commands and accessed the recording from the cameras on the front and kitchen doors, with both displays side by side on the monitor in front of him. It didn't take long to find what he was looking for.

He cursed and pressed a key to pause the footage. Then he shoved his gun into his holster.

"Detective Downing? What's going on?"

Chris forced a smile. Griffin was always polite, but for him to call Chris "Detective" meant he was getting really worried.

"It's okay, Griffin. Everything's okay. When I went to open the kitchen door to let you in, I realized the security alarm was off. I thought something might have happened, so I had to check things out. But everything is fine."

The look of relief that swept over the older man's

face was palpable. "Good, that is very good. Dillon will tease you about forgetting to set the alarm then." He grinned.

Chris smiled back. "Yeah, he'll get a kick out of that. Was there anything that you needed?"

"No, no. Just saw your truck, wanted to check on you and see about Miss Ashley. If you don't need me, I'll get back to work."

"Thanks, Griffin. Good to see you again."

"You, too."

As soon as Griffin left the room, Chris turned back to the monitor. It showed a picture of the front door opening a crack. From the inside. He pushed Play and the image expanded to show Julie Webb sneaking out the front door. Which meant she must have watched him key in the security code yesterday and she'd shut off the alarm.

He watched the video until she disappeared from the camera shot. He punched up several other videos, examining angles from other cameras. Then he turned off the monitors and pulled out his cell phone.

"You on your way?" Chief Thornton asked, recognizing Chris's cell phone number.

"Actually, no. There's something I need to take care of. It'll be a couple more hours before I can bring Julie to the station."

CHRIS DROVE HIS pickup across the field toward the weathered gray barn on the right side of Cooper's farm. The older man's white pickup was sitting beside the barn where he must have left it before going into the hospital. After last night, Chris had planned on calling someone else to clear the land he'd promised Cooper he'd clear. But after seeing the security video, and seeing Julie climb into the back of his pickup and hide under a tarp early this morning, he'd changed his mind.

He was going to make her tell him what she was hiding and why she'd snuck out of the house. To do that, he needed some time alone with her. His boss would think to check Harmony Haven if he got impatient waiting on him to bring Julie in. But he'd never think to look here. The only question now was how long Julie would let this little farce play out before she came out of hiding. She was about to find out that Chris could be a very patient man.

He parked next to the white pickup and killed his engine. He waited, checked the rearview mirror, waited some more. When the tarp didn't move, he let out an exasperated breath and hopped out of the truck, shoving the keys into his jeans pocket.

Two blood-bay mares and a palomino gelding idled lazily in the corral attached to the barn. Cooper's small farm was several miles from the nearest neighbor, but all of them were pitching in until he was back on his feet. One of them must have come by this morning already and fed and turned out the horses. That was the sum total of livestock on the farm. Cooper kept the horses for his grandkids when they came visiting. Otherwise, he rotated tobacco and hay in his fields, to augment his pension and keep himself from being bored.

Thousand-pound round bales of freshly cut orchard grass dotted the field behind the barn and the little one-story farmhouse a few hundred yards away. The grass was already drying to a golden brown that would become hay. In a few more days, another neighbor would bring equipment to gather up the bales. By the time Cooper was home, all he'd have to do was tend the summer garden he wanted for his own personal use. Which was why Chris was here.

Unless Julie quit being stubborn and made herself known, he'd be just as stubborn and go ahead and clear the acre of brush close to the house to make it easier for the owner to tend without having to walk so far. Cooper was getting a hip replacement, which meant exercise was good for him. But there was a limit to just how far he should have to walk and Chris aimed to help him out in that regard.

After another glance at his truck, he headed into the barn that housed Cooper's tractor and other farming equipment. He was just about to hook up the Bush Hog mower attachment to the back of the tractor when his phone vibrated. When he took it out of the holder and saw who was calling, a mixture of worry and dread shot through him.

"Dillon, did something happen? Are Ashley and the baby okay?"

A tired sigh sounded through the phone. "They're no worse than when you and I spoke earlier this morning. We're still fighting to keep the baby in the oven. Ashley's going stir-crazy, wanting to get out of bed. But the doctors won't let her move and they've been pumping her with meds to stop her contractions."

"Sorry, man. Is there anything I can do? Do you want me to bring something to the hospital?"

"You already have."

"What?"

"That ADA, Nelson? She sent two henchmen to the hospital an hour ago to ask me if I knew where you'd taken the witness. This is the first chance I've had to call and tell you."

Chris tightened his hands around the phone. "Henchmen? Are you talking about Henson and Bolton, her admin assistants? They should have gone back to Nashville with her."

"Well they didn't. I don't suppose you noticed they're both over six feet tall and built like bodyguards? You don't really think they're Nelson's gofers, do you?"

"Honestly, I'm embarrassed to say that I didn't pay them much attention at all last night. Other than noting they both had dark brown hair and wore matching gray suits, I probably couldn't pick them out of a lineup. I'm sorry they bothered you."

"Oh, I didn't let them bother me. When they knocked on Ashley's door and introduced themselves, I introduced them to hospital security and had them escorted outside. I didn't like the vibe I got from either of them. You might want to run a background check and see who they really are and why they're hanging with an assistant district attorney."

Chris leaned against the tractor. "You have a working theory?"

Dillon paused before continuing. "Not based on any facts. It's more of a feeling. I didn't trust them. Which makes me not trust Nelson, either. I think your next-door neighbor has landed you in the middle of something really bad. And since you're going to be my daughter's godfather, I just wanted to tell you to be careful."

Chris couldn't help grinning. "So, you're having a girl."

A chuckle sounded through the phone. "We'd planned on being surprised during the delivery, but they've been doing so many ultrasounds and check-ups that we really couldn't avoid finding out the gender. So, yeah. We're having a girl."

"That's great. Any ideas on names yet?"

"We don't want to jinx anything, so we're waiting on that. Taking it one hour at a time. The doctor wants the baby to cook at least a couple more weeks, if possible. Until delivery, Ashley's on complete bed rest."

"She's going to go nuts lying around that long."

"Tell me about it. Hey, Chris. Back to this Julie Webb person and the goons who showed up this morning. I watched them from the hospital room window when they left. They were in two separate cars, which seems odd enough since they're both allegedly from out of town on a business trip together. What was even odder was that both cars were muscle cars. What's that sound like to you?"

"Like you said earlier, bodyguards. But the ADA wasn't with them?"

"No sign of her," Dillon said.

"Which means they aren't guards. We're back to the henchman theory."

"Pretty much. Be careful, all right? I mean it. Watch your six."

He glanced at the barn's huge double doors, made large enough to accommodate the tractor, and thought about his truck outside—and what was *in* the truck— or rather, who. His little game of outwaiting Julie was no longer viable, not if there were two thugs looking for her. He pushed away from the tractor and headed toward the doors to get her out of her hiding place. The bush hogging would have to wait.

"Thanks, Dillon. I'll check back later."

He ended the call and pushed through the double doors, just in time to see Cooper's white pickup truck bumping across the field toward the road.

With Julie Webb in the driver's seat.

Chris swore and ran toward his truck. He skidded to a halt at the driver's-side door, his boots sliding in the dirt. The front left tire—which had cost a cool five hundred dollars because it was so big—was completely flat. He whirled around in time to see the white pickup reach the road and turn north toward town. A moment later, Julie had rounded a curve and thick stands of pine trees hid her from sight.

A whinny had Chris turning around. The palomino brushed against the corral fence, its head extended over the railing as it tore chunks of sweet clover out of the ground.

Chris ran into the barn. Less than a minute later, he had a harness and reins on the palomino. No time for a saddle. He led the gelding out of the corral, grabbed a fistful of mane and vaulted onto its back.

"Yah!" he yelled, squeezing his thighs against the horse. The gelding squealed and took off at a bone-jarring gallop across the field. Right before the horse reached the road, Chris yanked the reins, sending them both crashing into the woods.

Chapter Ten

Gravel seemed to roll beneath the wheels like a wave as Julie fought to keep the truck on the road. She eased her foot off the gas and the pickup straightened out. Too fast. She was going way too fast for these bumpy country roads. If she didn't slow down she'd end up in a ditch.

Easing off the accelerator even more, she glanced in her rearview mirror. She'd caught a glimpse of Chris running out of the barn when she'd stolen his friend's truck. Thank goodness she'd let the air out of one of his tires. Facing him when he looked that angry wasn't something she hoped to do anytime soon.

Guilt swept through her as she sped up again on a straightaway. From the moment she'd met her sexy neighbor, he'd been nothing but nice. He'd done everything he could to protect her. And how did she repay him? She'd snuck out of the house before dawn, using the security code that she'd seen him enter into the keypad when they'd gotten there. And then,

when she'd realized she was in the middle of nowhere with no hope of escaping on her own, she'd
hunkered down in the back of his four-by-four, hoping he wouldn't notice.

Her plan had worked. Except for the part where
he didn't take her into town and, instead, drove to a
farm even farther out in the boonies than the horse-
rescue place had been.

It didn't matter. Now that she had transportation,
she'd head to Destiny and leave the truck parked
somewhere obvious so the owner would find it. And
leave a wad of cash hidden inside as an apology for
taking it.

The trees seemed to encroach on the narrow road
as she slowed for another one of the hairpin turns.
At this rate, she might get there faster by walking.

She came out of the curve and onto another
straightaway. A dark blur suddenly burst from the
trees on the right and leaped onto the road fifty yards
ahead of her truck. A horse! She slammed the brakes
and desperately turned the wheel. The pickup began
to slide sideways like a jackknifed semi.

Oh, God, oh, God, oh, God. She was going to hit
the horse.

The animal gave a high-pitched whinny and
bolted toward the trees on the other side of the road
just as the pickup slid to a stop.

Julie's heart hammered in her chest, her breaths
coming in great gasps as she stared through the
windshield. Her hands gripped the steering wheel

so tightly she could feel her pulse thumping in her fingers.

What in the world had just happened?

She blinked, drew a ragged breath and scanned the road, looking for the horse. There, thirty feet away on the left, it stood with its head down, calmly munching on the tall green grass beside the road. Reins hung down from its harness. But it wasn't wearing a saddle. She frowned. Had someone been on the horse when it dashed in front of her? Everything had happened so fast. But she was almost positive she'd seen something, someone, bent low over the horse's neck.

Her door flew open. She jerked around and let out a squeal of alarm.

In the opening stood a very angry looking Chris Downing.

His dark eyes seemed almost black as he glared at her. "Get. Out."

CHRIS STALKED ACROSS the road toward the gelding, leaving Julie standing beside the truck, minus the keys this time, which Cooper had been foolish enough—or trusting enough—to leave in the cab. Then again, around these parts, people didn't make a habit of stealing their neighbors' vehicles. Unlocked doors were the norm. The only reason that Chris and Dillon were so security conscious was because in their role as police officers they saw more than the average citizen of the dangers that lurked out there.

Like from out of towners passing through, such as Julie Webb.

He cursed beneath his breath and forced himself to act as calmly as possible so he wouldn't spook the horse. He spoke to it in low, soothing tones as he took off the harness and scratched its velvety nose. Then he steered the horse around to the other side of the road and slapped its withers, sending it off at a trot back into the woods.

Julie's eyes widened as he strode toward her. She glanced at the harness in his hand, then the horse as it disappeared into the trees. He wasn't going to tell her that the horse would find its way back home just like a cat would. Let her wonder, and maybe worry just a bit about the havoc she'd caused.

He tossed the harness and reins in the bed of the truck and popped open the driver's door.

"Get in."

She glanced longingly toward the trees where the horse had gone, then at the road that led toward town.

"You just told me to get out."

He grabbed her around the waist and lifted her into the cab of the truck. Not giving her a chance to hop back out or argue with him, he climbed in after her, forcing her to slide over.

She glared at him and kept sliding, then grabbed the passenger-door handle.

Chris yanked her toward him and anchored her against his side with his arm around her shoulders.

"Let me go." Her eyes flashed with anger.

He leaned down until his face was just inches from hers, intentionally using his much larger size to get his point across.

"I'll let you go if you give me your word that you won't try to hop out of the truck."

A shiver went through her as she stared up at him, uncertainty replacing the anger in her eyes.

And just like that, Chris's own anger began to fade. Intimidating a young woman who'd been through what Julie had been through didn't make him exactly feel proud of himself. He swore yet again and released her.

"All you had to do was ask me to take you back to town and I would have." He shoved the keys in the ignition and started the engine. "Slashing a five-hundred-dollar tire and stealing my friend's truck was completely unnecessary."

She was silent as he did a three-point turn in the middle of the road and headed toward Cooper's farm.

"I didn't slash your tire."

He glanced at her.

"I just let the air out," she clarified. "I don't have a knife." She held out her hands in a placating gesture. "Not that I would have cut the tire if I'd had a knife. I just needed a head start. I didn't want to hurt anyone, or their property. I would have left this truck parked in town for the owner."

"The owner is in the hospital recovering from surgery. He doesn't need the stress of being told by someone that his one and only truck has been stolen and then found downtown. Why did you do it? Why did you sneak out of Dillon's house and then hide in the back of my truck, only to steal Cooper's truck and make a run for it? It's not like you were under arrest. And you have a phone, don't you? If you'd wanted a cab, you could have called for one."

She snorted and gave a little laugh. "I would have called a cab, but I forgot the name of your friend's farm. And the GPS on my phone couldn't figure out where I was. Apparently, that horse place doesn't exist in whatever maps my not-so-smart phone has."

He steered around another curve. "It's called Harmony Haven." He glanced at her. "Are you afraid of me?"

"What? Afraid of you? Why would you think that?"

He shook his head in exasperation. "You snuck away, stole a truck to avoid me. Call it a hunch."

This time it was her turn to roll her eyes. "Okay, okay. I may not completely trust you, but I trust you more than I've trusted anyone else for a long time. It's just that the longer I sat in that guest room thinking about the questions you'd be asking me in the morning, the more I realized I didn't want to involve you further. This is my battle. Not yours."

He turned onto the long dirt driveway up to Cooper's farmhouse. When he reached the house, he threw the truck into Park but left the engine running to keep the cab cool. The summer heat was already uncomfortable even this early in the morning.

Turning to face her, he put his right arm across the back of the bench seat.

"Let me see if I have this all straight in my mind. Your husband tried to kill you—twice. I'm the police officer who had to kill him to save you. I think I'm already involved almost as deep as I can be."

Her face flushed a light pink. "Well, when you put it that way, it does sound like too little, too late. But at least I can protect you from here on out by not involving you anymore."

"What part of *I'm a police officer* did you not hear? Julie, I'm a detective and part-time SWAT officer. It's my job to protect you, and to find out what's going on, administrative leave or not. And if you're still in any danger, it's my job to figure out why and who is after you."

Her eyes widened.

He shook his head and let out a deep sigh. "I've been a cop since I got out of college thirteen years ago. I can read body language. And right now yours is screaming that you think there's more to your husband's attempts on your life than typical domestic violence, if there is such a thing as typical in these cases."

When she didn't say anything, he shut the engine off and shoved his door open. "Come on. At least let me take you inside while we talk this out. And, once we do, if you still want to go into town, I'll take you myself. In *my* truck."

She didn't agree with his plan, but she didn't try to run either. He supposed that was progress.

They were heading toward the front porch when the sound of galloping hooves reached them. He immediately shoved her behind his back and drew his gun. The palomino gelding appeared around the corner, tossing its mane and blowing out a snort as it stopped a few feet from him.

Chris holstered the gun and opened the front door.

"Go on in," he said. When she didn't move, he added, "Please?"

She hesitated, then stepped inside.

Chris started to pull the door shut but she stopped him with a hand on his.

"What are you doing?" she asked.

"I'm going to put the horse back in the corral. I'll be right back."

Chapter Eleven

A few minutes later, Julie sat at the kitchen table in Cooper's house, watching a shirtless Chris sit down across from her. His shirt had been soaked with sweat from his ride on the horse, so he'd washed it out in the sink and hung it on a chair to dry. He'd also rinsed his hair under the faucet. Julie had freshened up in the bathroom as much as possible without taking a real shower. And now she was desperately trying to pretend he wasn't completely distracting her.

His thick hair was beginning to dry in waves of cinnamon brown that made her fingers itch to touch it. But far more enticing was his golden-skinned, impressively muscled chest.

Chris Downing had a mouthwatering body to go along with his handsome face. And she was in no way immune to his appeal. The only thing keeping her from blatantly staring at the dips and valleys of his muscular chest and abs was the fact that he was grilling her with questions—questions that were going a long way toward dampening her enthusiasm for the incredible male specimen sitting across from her.

He'd asked her to give him more details about her husband attacking her five months ago. She told him about that night and that right after he'd paid bail, he'd disappeared, gone off grid, only communicating through his lawyer. Which had left Julie looking over her shoulder all the time, worried he'd try to come back and finish what he'd started.

"The first month after he disappeared, things were okay. But then his family filed a civil suit, alleging I was lying about the attack. And little things started happening, like someone slashing my tires. I was convinced that either Alan, or his family, was harassing me. The ADA's office didn't have the budget to offer 24/7 protection, which I needed if I was going to stay in Nashville. Since most of my accounts have been frozen as a result of the civil case, I can't afford that kind of security, either. So I'd moved here until the criminal case against my husband was settled, or until I had to go back to fight the civil case. I was trying to keep a low profile."

"That worked out really well," Chris said, his tone dry. "Why do you think your husband's family is suing you? Sounds to me like there's plenty of evidence against your husband."

"Kathy said it's a device to try to undermine the criminal case against him."

Chris nodded. "The threshold for proof in a civil case is much lower than in a criminal case. A civil judgment could sway the media in their favor, maybe turn a juror, even though they're supposed to ignore things like that.

He tapped a hand on the table. "So the reason you called the ADA after the shooting is because of the criminal case? To keep Nelson in the loop?"

She nodded. "That and I really didn't know anyone else to call. It's not like I have a lawyer on retainer. I wanted her advice, and she immediately said she was on her way."

"Awfully nice of her."

"I guess."

He studied her for a moment. "What were you and your husband arguing about when he found you in Destiny?"

"Arguing?"

"I heard you scream, twice, heard voices raised in argument before I confronted your husband. The screams, I get. He threatened you, cut you with the knife. But what was it that you were fighting about?"

"I remember he was angry that I'd shot him in Nashville, and that I ran away, as he called it. He threatened me, grabbed my arm, shook me. I probably cried out when he did that. Mostly I just kept telling him to go away and leave me alone."

He stared at her as if he didn't believe her. She tried to remember what she and Alan were saying when Chris had barged into the house. But she'd been so scared. The angry words they'd exchanged were all jumbled up in her mind.

"The last time he confronted you, you shot him. Was he worried about a gun this time?" Chris asked.

"I don't have a gun. I had to surrender it as evidence when the police arrived at my home that night."

"Did your husband know that?"

"Probably. We never talked about... I can't be sure. Actually, I seem to remember him asking if I had my gun. So, yeah, I guess he was concerned about it."

Some of the suspicion seemed to leave his face, as if he'd been testing her and she'd passed. What would happen if she hadn't passed?

"Did he have the knife with him when he came inside? Did he take it from the kitchen? Or did he take it from you?"

So much for him not being suspicious anymore. "What are you talking about?"

"Are you the one who had the knife first? Did your husband wrestle it away from you?"

"I never had the knife."

"Then we won't find your fingerprints on it?"

She held her hands out to her sides. "I don't know."

"You don't know?" He sounded incredulous.

"When I came out of my bedroom, Alan was standing there, holding the knife. I don't know if he brought it with him or grabbed it from my kitchen."

"You have to know what knives you brought with you when you rented the house. Judging by all the boxes I saw, you didn't have time to unpack before your husband got there."

"True, I didn't get to unpack everything. But I did unpack the boxes for the kitchen. I was looking forward to preparing my first decent meal since arriving in Destiny. I really don't know whether he'd grabbed one of my knives or brought his own."

"What were you arguing about?" he asked again, barely giving her a chance to catch her breath between questions.

"I told him to leave me alone. Why are you badgering me?"

"Because things aren't adding up. If your husband's goal was to kill you, he'd have snuck up on you, stabbed or shot you before you even knew he was there. Instead, he confronted you. So here's the real question. What do you have that your husband wanted so badly that he was willing to risk getting killed?"

Chapter Twelve

Chris checked his shirt hanging over the kitchen chair beside him. It was finally dry enough to wear, so he pulled it over his head and smoothed it into place.

"I think Alan might have been talking about the key to the safe," Julie said from her seat across from him.

"Safe? What safe?"

"When Alan and I separated, about nine months ago, I had all the locks changed while he was at work. He'd been angry, moody, aggressive—like, in your face aggressive but never actually hitting me. I'd never seen him like that before and it scared me. So I got a restraining order. And had the locks changed. That made him even angrier. Over the months that followed, he kept calling. He would say he needed different things from the house. Every time he'd mention something, I'd pack it up and ship it to his apartment. But he was never satisfied. It seemed like he was making excuses to try to get me to let him come over. That whole back and forth arguing went on for four months. Then he broke in one night and you know the rest."

"Was there a specific incident that made you separate from him nine months ago?"

She considered his question, then shrugged. "More like a series of them. In the first years of our marriage, he never mentioned my family. But this past year, he started bringing them up for seemingly no reason. He asked if I had anything to remember them by. I told him I had what mattered, memories. That seemed to make him really angry. Then I said all I had of them, physically, was a box of pictures and junk. He demanded that I show him what I had. If he hadn't acted so odd, I probably would have. But he'd been acting so strange, I refused. He went ballistic. The next day I changed the locks."

"You mentioned a safe. Is that where you put this box?"

"No. The pictures, costume jewelry, Naomi's hair clips, my dad's baseball cards—they're all in a safety deposit box that I haven't opened since their deaths. The safe I'm talking about is in our house in Nashville. When Alan broke into my house here in Destiny yesterday, after calling me vile names and ranting about the shooting and me leaving, at some point he demanded that I give him the key."

"What key?" Chris asked.

"I was about to ask him the same thing when you came in and things spiraled out of control. I got the impression he had a lot more he wanted to say. But he never got a chance. If he thought I had something in the safe that belonged to him, he was wrong. The thing is, I filed for divorce after Alan attacked me. And I gave him everything that was listed in the pending divorce decree, on top of what I'd already given him. So all I can figure is that he lost something, maybe some important papers that he didn't want anyone to know about. I'm not sure. But, like you said, it had to be important. It just occurred to me that he might have been talking about the floor safe in the house in Nashville. It was there when we bought the place and I remember him saying it would be a good place to keep our birth certificates and passports, things like that. But then I forgot about it. I never used that safe, but maybe he did. And maybe he thought I had the key."

"Do you?"

She shrugged. "I honestly don't know. Alan was practically a hoarder. I was all about keeping things neat and simple. Any time he left stuff lying around the house I'd put it up. It's very likely if he left a key somewhere that I might have thrown it in a junk drawer. But even if he thought I had the key, wouldn't it be easier for him to break into the house and try to, I don't know, pick the lock? Seems crazy that he'd track me down out here just for a key."

"It probably depends on what's in the safe, if indeed that's why he came here. Floor safes are generally extremely heavy and require special equipment to install. He couldn't have just broken into your house and taken the safe with him. And unless he's a master lock-picker, he'd need a locksmith to help him break into the thing. It would be hard for him to get a professional locksmith to pick the front door lock and a safe lock. They'd know something was up and would probably call the police."

She nodded. "When you put it that way, I suppose that coming here might be worth the risk—if we're even going down the right path. There could have been another reason entirely for him coming here. But that's the only key I can think of."

"Have you told Nelson about the safe?"

She shook her head. "Why would I? You asking me about what Alan said is the only reason I thought of it now."

"Don't."

She frowned. "Don't tell the ADA? Why?"

"How well do you know her?"

"Again, why?"

"Because she's the one who told you to leave town, to hide so your husband wouldn't find you. And yet, he did. Besides her, who knew you were here, in Destiny?"

She grew very still. "There isn't anyone else. Kathy is the only person I told. But she wouldn't tell Alan where I was. Kathy is the one who's been helping me fight him in court."

"Then how did your husband find you?"

"You're the detective. You tell me."

Her sarcasm and obvious frustration had him

smiling. He was pushing her hard, probably harder than the chief would have if she were back at the station undergoing an official interview. But this was probably his only chance to ask her questions before turning her over to the team, and he intended to get as many answers as he could.

"Did you come directly to Destiny after leaving Nashville?" he asked.

"No. I wasn't sure where to hideout. I drove around the state, checking out several small towns before settling on this one. It took me about a week of exploring to decide that Destiny was where I wanted to land."

"The car you drove here, is it yours?"

"It's mine."

"How have you bought gas and food since leaving your home?"

"All cash. I've seen enough TV crime shows to know not to leave an electronic trail."

He nodded. "Good. How did you lease the house here in Destiny?"

"Cash again. I saw the place in an ad, called the number, met the landlord in person, paid cash and signed a fake name." Her face flushed a light red. "Probably not legal, exactly, but again I was worried about Alan being able to find me. I suppose if the landlord had pushed for ID I'd have been in trouble. But he didn't."

"Around here, people aren't as suspicious as they

might be in a big city. You never answered my question about Nelson. How well do you know her?"

"We're casual friends, just barely. I met her and Alan a couple of months into my senior year in college." Some kind of emotion flashed in her eyes. Sorrow? Pain?

"You okay?" he asked.

She drew a bracing breath. "Yes, sorry. Just… thinking. Anyway, I…was…having a tough time in school and pretty much kept to myself. Kathy was in one of my classes. I knew her name but that was about it. I think she took pity on me. We started hanging out every once in a while. One day, I guess she could see how down I was and she insisted that I go to the school's football game that night. She had an extra ticket because a friend had canceled. When we got there, we sat by Alan. Neither of us knew him, but he introduced himself and we got to know each other a bit during the game. After that, we'd occasionally go to movies or other college events."

"So it's fair to say the three of you became friends?"

"More like acquaintances than friends. I clicked pretty well with Alan and Kathy, but they were like oil and water with each other. She tolerated him but didn't really like him. I tried to stay friends with both of them, but Alan and I got serious pretty fast. He… helped me through a really tough time. And, well, when you're guy-crazy you sometimes forget about your other friends. Kathy and I didn't ever get very close because I was usually with Alan. We got married right after graduation. Or, well, my graduation anyway. Alan had failed a few courses and never finished his degree. After I graduated, he stopped taking classes and decided to go into his family's business, Webb Enterprises." She waved her hand. "Not that any of that is relevant."

Chris didn't want to assume anything wasn't relevant at this point, but he did have other questions he wanted to ask right now. "Did Nelson attend your wedding?"

"No. We didn't invite her." Her cheeks flushed a light pink. "It's embarrassing now to say that. I mean, she was a friend, even if we weren't really close. But like I said, Alan didn't like her. So, no invitation. I guess you'd say I chose Alan over her."

"Maybe you only thought she and Alan didn't get along. Maybe she liked him and resented you. After all, you did both meet him at the same football game."

She shook her head. "She was never anything but kind to me, never expressed any resentment. And Alan never looked twice at her. She wasn't his type."

She held up her hands as if to stop him from arguing. "Before you say it, I know—she's tall and blonde, which most guys like, while I'm short and a brunette. But even if he and Kathy had been able to get along, he just wasn't attracted to women like her, with her kind of forceful personality. Everything about her set him off, irritated him. And he showed me pictures of some of his former girlfriends. Every one of them was like me—short, brunette."

Chris could certainly see Julie's appeal over the glossier, more made-up look that Kathy Nelson sported. Nelson was sophisticated but seemed fake, whereas Julie seemed the girl-next-door type, a beautiful girl next door but still down to earth, approachable. Still, that didn't mean Alan couldn't have been attracted to both of them.

"If neither of you kept up with Nelson, then why is she so invested in your case that she drove all the way out here from Nashville?"

"We didn't keep up with her at all. The first time I had seen her since college was the night that Alan was arrested. And the reason she's taking this case so personally is because Alan is…was… something of a celebrity in Nashville. He comes from money. His family is well-known in high-society circles and he was a respected philanthropist. Kathy is a career muckety-muck looking for a way into the governor's office. She made no secret to me that she felt if she could win against someone as high profile as Alan Webb, she'd prove she was in nobody's pocket and was tough on crime. She'd make a name for herself and be well on her way to establishing her political career."

That part didn't surprise Chris at all. Even in Destiny, people had heard of Kathy Nelson and her political aspirations. But there might have been another reason, too. If Julie was wrong—if Kathy did like Alan and felt he'd chosen Julie over her—maybe being in charge of the case against him was a way to get even for him passing her over in college. That seemed unlikely, though, to hold that kind of a grudge over three years later. Especially since Kathy was married.

Chris made a mental note to check with his team to see if they were looking into Kathy as a potential suspect. Just to cover the bases.

"Let's get back to the night your husband attacked you in Nashville. When was that?"

"About five months ago, on my twenty-fifth birthday."

A sick feeling twisted in Chris's gut. "Not that there's a good day to try to kill you, but on your birthday? Really?"

"Yes. Really." She was twisting her hands together again. "Like I said earlier, we'd been separated for about four months. Looking back now, the marriage was never what I'd hoped it would be. He'd doted on me in college. But as soon as that ring was on my finger, things cooled off, changed. At first, I thought it was because he'd quit school and took over the family business. He was under a lot of stress. And I figured he was frustrated that he never got to work in the field he loved."

"What field was that?"

"Botany. He absolutely loved working with plants. He could talk for hours about their medicinal properties and how to get more yield from organically grown crops. He'd planned on having his own career for a while before having to take the reins of the company. But it didn't work out that way. He's an only child, and his father's health was failing. He had to step in much sooner than he'd hoped. Once he started working at Webb Enterprises, that's when he started getting depressed and closing himself off from me. Then again, maybe I'm making up excuses for him. Maybe it was just me he didn't like."

The hurt was there again, in the tightening of her jaw, the way her lips thinned. She'd loved her husband once upon a time—that was obvious. And even now, she couldn't fathom why he'd turned on her.

Neither could Chris.

Why had Alan tried to kill her? Twice?

She waved her hands again, as if waving away her words. "Shortly before we separated, I remember him coming home one night in a sour mood after work and shutting himself up in his office for hours. Wouldn't even come out for dinner. And once he did emerge, it was almost as if…as if he were a different person. He was…serious, angry. He insisted that I call in the next day and take a week's vacation, said we needed to get away. I couldn't just drop everything like that. People count on me." She twisted her hands. "At least, they used to. I had to quit work once the media got hold of the story about Alan attacking me and me shooting him. I became a liability to my coworkers at that point."

"Where did you work?"

She hesitated, looked away. "I started a nonprofit foundation, figured it was a good use of my business management degree and I could help people. The office was in downtown Nashville. We fought to raise awareness and money to fight orphan diseases—illnesses that are so rare that it isn't profitable enough for a drug company to devote money researching possible cures or even treatments. But the diseases are devastating to the victims and their families."

He studied her. Her voice was a little too bright, like the emotion was forced. She was hiding something. He'd sensed it from the moment she'd begun talking about the tough time she'd been having right before she'd met Alan. There'd been a flash of pain in her eyes then, the same flash of pain in her eyes right now.

"Julie?"

"Hmm?" She was staring toward the front window, at the acres of green grass that would need mowing soon.

"What was the name of the nonprofit?"

She swallowed hard. "Naomi's Hope Foundation."

Again, she wouldn't look at him. And then he got it.

"Was Naomi a friend or a family member?"

Her startled gaze shot to his. She stared at him so long he thought she wasn't going to answer. But then she sighed heavily, looking defeated.

"She was my sister, a year older than me. My parents went broke taking her to hospitals, flying around the country to different specialists. They even went down to Mexico once, looking into alternative medicines. Nothing helped. She had a condition so rare it didn't even have a name. It baffled every doctor who tried to treat her. It struck her during her senior year in college, my junior year at the same school. She died four months later. At least she wasn't in pain anymore. She was free. But my parents…"

She shook her head. "They were immigrants, my mom and dad. Star-crossed lovers from London. Both sets of their parents, my grandparents, didn't approve of them dating. So as soon as they were of legal age, they married and moved to this country. They left their families, their history, everything familiar to them to have a fresh start, to build a legacy of their own. They were Romeo and Juliet, basically, coming here for the American dream.

"They didn't have any money, their families had disowned them and they had to fight for everything they had, which was never much. Their entire life savings was built around sending Naomi and me to college. But when Naomi…" She shook her head. "Naomi was a daddy's girl. When she died, my father couldn't handle it. He shot himself. The day after his funeral, my mother took an overdose of sleeping pills and alcohol."

Tears were running down her face now. Her bottom lip trembled.

"I always wondered what went through their minds when they did it. I know they were devastated. We all were. But, somewhere along the way, they forgot they had another daughter. They left me all alone. I had no one to turn to. But I couldn't let their sacrifices be for nothing. Naomi died in the summer after my junior year, my parents right after that. A month later I enrolled for the fall session of my senior year. I felt I owed it to my parents to get my degree. But I was miserable, couldn't concentrate on my studies. A couple of months later, I was about ready to give up. And that's when I met Alan. He turned my life around. He was there for me, encouraged me. And then he...then he..."

She covered her face with her hands, her shoulders shaking as her misery overtook her.

Chris stood and crossed to her. He couldn't bear doing nothing, so he took a chance and damned the consequences. He pulled her to standing and wrapped his arms around her.

"I'm so sorry, Julie," he whispered, resting his cheek against the top of her head. "I'm so very, very sorry."

She'd stiffened when he first touched her. But then she seemed to melt against him, putting her arms around his waist and clinging to him while tears tracked down her face, soaking his shirt.

They stood there a long time while he whispered soothing words against her hair. The storm finally subsided, her tears stopped and she was no longer shaking.

Finally, with one last sniffle, she pushed back and gave him a watery smile. "Thank you."

The pain in her beautiful blue eyes had him wanting to pull her back into his arms. But he fought the urge and instead allowed himself only to gently push her tousled hair out of her eyes, then wipe the last of her tears from her cheeks before dropping his hands to his sides.

"Anytime." He smiled and stepped back to put some much-needed space between them.

She drew a shaky breath. "I don't think my heart or your shirt can take much more of this. You might as well finish asking your questions right now."

"We don't have to—"

"Yes. We do," she said. "I want to know why Alan did what he did. And you need the investigation resolved. Both of us need this case closed in order to get on with our lives. So go on. Ask whatever else you want to know."

"All right. What about the movers?"

"Movers?" She frowned. "What about them?"

"Yesterday afternoon, they brought your furniture and belongings. I assume they drove down from Nashville. Did you pay them cash, too? Or did you use a credit card when you hired them?"

"I went to the bank the day I left and withdrew several thousand dollars from my checking account so I could live on cash for a while. I paid the movers in cash like I did everything else."

"Several thousand dollars—from checking, not

savings?" he asked. "I'm not exactly living paycheck to paycheck, but I'd have to dip into savings to pull out several thousand in cash."

"Even with the civil suit freezing our joint accounts, I still have plenty of money in my personal accounts. As long as I'm not too extravagant, I'll be okay until the case is settled. Money has never been a problem for Alan and me. Like I said, he took over the family business, an import/export empire. Even without receiving his botany degree, he'd taken enough classes in his minor—business management—to do really well running the company. And he was smart, really smart. The company was struggling when the economy went south. But within weeks of Alan taking it over, the profits soared."

That didn't sound right to Chris. A young kid, freshly flunked out of college, was able to turn around the family business? A lot of things about Alan didn't sound right. The next time Chris called his boss he was going to see how the background check on Julie's former husband was going. He wanted a complete history on Alan Webb, from birth to the grave.

Julie shoved her chair up to the table and remained standing, wrapping her arms around her waist. "That's what allowed me to work at the non-profit instead of getting a job that paid real money. I'd offered to work at his family's business, to help him manage it. But he didn't want me to worry about that, insisted that I chase my dream of getting the government to devote resources to research orphan diseases like my sister's. It truly was the most decent thing he ever did."

The bitterness in her voice told him there was a lot more water under the matrimonial bridge, but he decided to steer clear of that for now. Making her miserable wasn't his goal. He'd only delve into that earlier line of questioning again if it was absolutely necessary.

"All right. Back to the moving company then. I'm surprised they took cash. Most companies like that require a credit card."

"Yeah, well. You'd be surprised what a few hundred dollars under the table can do for you."

"You bribed them."

"I did what I had to do to stay under the radar. It's not like Alan was involved in some kind of nefarious criminal activity and the government was giving me a new identity to testify against him. He was just a husband who'd tried to murder his wife. I was on my own. I would have used a fake name if I could. But they required ID, wouldn't budge on that. So, as soon as I decided that I wanted to leave Nashville, I had them put the things I would need into storage and left everything else in the house to deal with at a later time. Like I said before, about a week later I knew where I wanted to settle. After renting the place in Destiny, I called them to arrange a date and time for them to deliver my things."

"There's a direct link from your house to the

moving company to here if someone wanted to follow it. That could be how Alan tracked you. But
it's not like he could have watched the storage unit
24/7. He had to sleep sometime. If the movers had
loaded up the unit while Alan was asleep, he'd have
missed that link to you and wouldn't have been able
to find you—assuming that he did find you through
the movers. I'm betting he had a partner. He wasn't
working alone in his quest to locate you." He studied her carefully. "And you're not surprised by that.
Why not?"

She shrugged. "When your husband tries to kill
you, trying to figure out why he wants you dead
pretty much consumes your thoughts. The fact that
he found me so fast this second time shocked me.
And it made me think he had to be working with
someone else. He had to have help. And I couldn't see
him hiring a private investigator, not with the criminal case hanging over his head. That could look bad
in court. Like he was stalking me. I figure it has to
be someone bad, a criminal, someone likely as dangerous as Alan became. So, no, it doesn't surprise
me. I figured he had a partner. The only question is
who, and of course, whether they still want me dead
now that Alan's gone."

Listening to the pain in her voice, the confusion
and anger pretty much obliterated his earlier concerns that she might have intentionally used him as
a tool to kill her husband. She was consistent in her
answers. She didn't hesitate like she would if she was

making up lies as she went along. And her body language struck him as honest, too. He'd bet all of his years of experience at interviewing witnesses that everything she was telling him now was true.

Or at least what she thought was true. But there was still one more thing bugging him.

"Have you told me everything?" he asked.

"Yes, of course."

"Then why are you still running? Why stow away in the back of my truck, and steal Cooper's truck, to get away from me if you've done nothing wrong and have nothing to hide? You said you think your husband has a partner who might be after you. So why wouldn't you trust the policeman who risked his own life to save you yesterday? It doesn't make sense, unless the real reason you want to be on your own is because you want to get even."

She blinked. "Excuse me?"

"You don't want some cop hanging around when you figure out who was working with Alan against you. Because you want revenge."

"That's ridiculous. I want to be safe, that's what I want."

"Then why run from me? I can protect you."

"I've known you for all of two seconds," she said, her voice shaking with anger. "I knew Alan for three and a half years, was married to him for three of those years. You tell me. Why should I trust you when I couldn't trust him?"

And that was the last piece of the puzzle he'd been

looking for. It had been in front of him all along. He'd quit thinking of her as a conspirator and was thinking of her solely as a victim. But he still hadn't understood why she'd run. It all came down to trust. She'd been hurt, horribly hurt, and here he was berating her for not being willing to put her faith and her life in his hands when, as she'd said, she'd known him for all of "two seconds."

He'd been a complete ass and hadn't even realized it.

"Julie."

When she didn't reply, he moved a step closer and took her hand in his. She tried to tug it away, but he held fast.

"Julie, maybe you don't trust me completely yet. I get that. I understand it after everything you've been through. But look at this objectively. We both want the same thing. We want answers. The answer to why Alan tried to kill you—twice—will enable you to go back and live your life without having to look over your shoulder and worry that someone else is out there trying to hurt you. That same answer will help me resolve this case so I can go back to my life, to being a cop. We both want the same thing, to end this. So how about we work together, as a team, and end this once and for all."

He could see the indecision on her face, in the way she chewed her bottom lip as if debating her options. For a moment, he thought she'd turn and walk away. But then, very slowly, she put her hand in his.

He couldn't help but notice how soft her skin was and how good it felt to thread his fingers with hers. And from the way her blue eyes widened at the contact, he had a feeling she was thinking much the same thing—that it was nice holding his hand, too.

A tiny red circle of light appeared on her forehead.

He shouted a warning and yanked her toward him just as the front window exploded in a hail of rifle fire.

Chapter Thirteen

"Stay down." Chris yanked his gun out of his holster.

Julie couldn't have gotten up if she wanted to, not with two-hundred pounds of protective male squashing her against the hardwood floor.

He rolled off her and jumped up in a half crouch, sprinting toward the window with his gun out in front of him.

Bam! Bam! Bam!

He fired through the gaping hole that used to be the front window, then dove toward the floor. Whoever was shooting at them outside let loose with another round of shots.

Julie covered her ears and squeezed her eyes shut. Bits of plaster and wood rained down where the bullets strafed the walls above her. When the chaos of noise and dust had settled, Chris was once again crouching over her, his gun pointed up at the ceiling. In his other hand was his phone.

"You okay?" he asked her.

She felt as if she'd inhaled a lungful of plaster

dust, but nodded to let him know she was at least alive. As for "okay," she'd reserve judgment on that.

"It's Chris," he said into the phone. "I'm over at Cooper's farm, holed up in the house with Julie Webb. We're taking rifle fire."

Julie looked toward the shattered front window while Chris talked police codes that made no sense to her. This low to the floor, she couldn't see the road or even the acres of grass outside. All she could see was the wall of trees at the edge of the cleared portion of the property. Where was the shooter? Was he making his way toward the house even now? Ready to lean in through the opening and gun them down?

She should have been terrified, melting into a puddle of tears and nerves. And maybe if this was the first time someone had tried to kill her, she would have been. But after everything she'd been through, and everything she'd lost, the only emotion flowing through her veins right now was rage.

She was absolutely livid.

If the shooter did lean in through that window, she'd try to tear him apart, limb by limb, with her bare hands. Assuming he didn't shoot her first, of course. She was so sick of people trying to hurt her. And what about Chris? Once again his life was in danger because someone had decided to go after her, or at least that was what she had to assume. It made sense that between the two of them, she was the target. And here Chris was in the wrong place at the wrong time, again.

"Give me your backup gun," she snapped, as he ended his call.

"My backup gun?"

If their situation wasn't so dire, she'd have laughed at the stunned look on his face.

"You do have one, right? All the cops in movies and on TV have them. It's probably strapped to your ankle. I may not be an expert marksman, but I do know how to shoot. I've been to gun ranges. I want to help."

He said something under his breath and she was pretty sure she didn't want to know what it was from the exasperated expression on his face.

"Unless you have law enforcement or military experience that I don't know about, I'll keep my alleged backup gun where it belongs. Come on. You can help us by getting out of the line of fire so I don't have to worry about you. Our friend out there is going to get braver anytime now and I don't want you catching a bullet when he does."

"Or she."

He nodded. "Or she. Come on."

He crouched over her, shielding her body with his as he duck walked with her out of the main room and down a short hallway. No more gunshots sounded from outside, which had her even more nervous. Judging by his worried look, it made him nervous, too.

"In here." He pushed her through a doorway into a bathroom.

An old-fashioned claw-foot tub sat against the far wall, beneath a small, high window.

"Get in."

He didn't wait for her to figure out what he meant before he was lifting her and settling her inside the tub.

"This is cast iron. It's the best protection from stray bullets that I can give you."

The idea of bullets ripping through the walls hadn't even occurred to her. The anger that had helped her stay calm earlier began to fade, leaving her shaking so hard her teeth chattered.

"Wh-what a-bout you?" she asked between chatters. "Sh-shouldn't you g-get in, too?"

He'd been half-standing, peeking through the bottom of the window. But when she spoke he ducked down, an amused, half smile curving his lips.

"As much as I'd love to join you in the tub," he teased, "the timing isn't right." He added an outrageous wink and even managed a chuckle.

She couldn't believe he was flirting with her at a time like this—or that she found him utterly charming. She was about to tell him to knock it off and get into the tub with her before he got shot, when the sound of gunfire echoed through the house.

Chris dove to the floor.

A loud pinging noise had Julie throwing her hands over her ears and squeezing her eyes shut. The shots seemed to go on forever. When they finally stopped, she lay there, her breaths coming in great gasps, her hands still covering her ears.

Forcing her eyes open, she pulled herself up to sitting. Sunlight slanted through small round holes riddling the outside wall. Paint chips lay scattered on the floor—the same color as the tub. That pinging sound she'd heard must have been a bullet hitting the tub. And she'd been safe, just as Chris had promised.

But where was he?

She looked through the open door into the hall-way, but it didn't have any windows and was too dark for her to see anything.

"Chris," she whispered, not wanting the shooter to hear her if he was close by. "Chris? Where are you?"

No one answered. No footsteps sounded on the hardwood floor from the other rooms. Had he left her? Alone?

She swallowed, hard, trying to tamp down the ris-ing panic that had her pulse hammering in her ears. It was too quiet outside. Had Chris gone out there to confront the shooter? Had he been forced to dive into the hallway to avoid getting shot, only to catch a stray bullet? If he was lying past the open door-way, injured, he could be bleeding out right now. She couldn't sit here and do nothing. She had to check on him, and if he was hurt, somehow she had to help him.

Her whole body shook as she started to pull her-self up on her knees in the tub. Something shifted against her leg and she let out a squeal of surprise before she could stop herself. She looked down. Chris hadn't left her alone, after all.

He'd left her his backup gun.

CHRIS EDGED HIS way around the back of the house, pistol sweeping out in front of him. He kept to the grass to make as little noise as possible. Leaving Julie alone inside had nearly killed him. But as soon as the bullets started coming through the wall, he knew it was only a matter of time before the shooter breached the house. Julie had a much better chance of survival if Chris could intercept the shooter outside.

She'd have an even better chance if his SWAT team would get here.

He checked his watch. It had only been ten minutes since he'd called them. Donna, Colby and Randy had probably been at church, which was a good half hour away. Max usually went to the evening service like Chris. But Max lived even farther out than the First Baptist Church. Hopefully, his team was speeding toward him like a moonshiner running from a revenue officer. Still, best case, the first of them might arrive in another ten minutes.

He and Julie didn't have ten minutes—not against someone with a rifle and a laser scope.

He ducked down and peered around the corner of the house. The side yard was empty and he couldn't see anyone out front. But thick trees to his right marched all the way down to the gravel road. There were a million places for someone with a rifle to hide. If Chris couldn't reach cover, and get up close and personal with the shooter, his 9mm was just about useless. What he needed was a way to draw the gunman out and keep him away from the house, and Julie.

He eased back behind the wall, glancing toward the barn, his truck, the corral with the horses. They were nervous, agitated, running back and forth because of the gunfire. Too dangerous to try capturing one, let alone riding it to create some kind of diversion—assuming he could even make it that far without being picked off by the rifle. No, he needed something else to get the gunman's attention.

His gaze slid to the large silver propane tank set about fifty yards back from the house. It was slightly toward the right side of the property, close to one of the round hay bales drying in the sun. Acres and acres of wide-open field with more hay bales opened off to the right. And, past that, the barn and the horses— far enough away that they would be safe from harm, but close enough that the animals would be terrified and make their own racket. Dillon and Ashley would kill him for even considering what he was about to do. But he figured three traumatized horses in exchange for saving Julie's life was a bargain he was willing to make.

To his left, a deadly sprint from the house, the line of thick pine trees and oaks beckoned as cover—*if* he could reach them. Then he could circle around, locate the shooter and end this dangerous stand-off.

He raised his pistol and aimed it at the propane tank. *Bam! Bam!*

Chris jerked around at the sound of gunfire to his right. Julie was crouching in the back doorway, shooting toward the closest round hay bale. The long end of a rifle appeared at the left side, pointed right at her.

"Get back!" Chris squeezed off several shots toward the rifleman to give Julie cover to head inside.

But, instead of running into the house, she ran toward him, her eyes wide, face pale.

Wood siding exploded close to her head. Chris fired toward the hay bale again and ran toward Julie. The rifle jerked back. Chris grabbed Julie around the waist and shoved her down against the foundation of the house while he kept his gun aimed toward the hay.

"You need to get back into the house," he hissed, without turning around. "Get into the cast-iron tub until I take this jerk down!"

"Can't." She sounded out of breath. "I was worried you were hurt or needed help and was coming to look for you when the front door creaked open. Someone else is inside."

The rifle shoved through the hay. Chris and Julie both started shooting. Julie's gun clicked empty.

As soon as the rifle jerked back, Chris reloaded.

"I need more bullets." Julie ejected the spent magazine like a pro and held out her hand.

"The extra ammo for that gun is in my truck."

She gave him an aggravated look that would have made him laugh at any other time. Most people he knew in this situation would be cowering in fear. Not Julie. She was full of surprises.

A hollow echo sounded from inside the house. Whoever was in there was probably searching for Julie. If they came out back, the two of them were done for. They had to get to cover—now.

He grabbed her around the waist, jerking her up to standing and pointing her toward the trees.

She instinctively tried to crouch back down against the house. Chris pulled her up again.

"Run," he ordered. "I'll cover you. Get to the trees. Go!"

She took off running.

The rifle shoved through the hay. Chris fired off several shots, drawing the rifle bore toward him. Bullets pinged against the house right beside him. He swore and dove to the side. The sound of running feet sounded from inside the house, coming toward the back door. In desperation, Chris swept his pistol toward the propane tank and squeezed the trigger.

An explosion of heat and sound engulfed him, knocking him backward. His skull cracked against the wood siding, making his vision blur. He shook his head, trying to focus. A wall of thick black smoke and flames blasted toward him, offering him much-needed cover. Pushing away from the house, he took off in a wobbly run toward the trees.

Chapter Fourteen

Julie peered around the same tree as Chris, looking toward the house and the burning remnants of the propane tank.

"I think the explosion took out the rifleman," Chris said. "The hay bale where he was hiding is obliterated. The question is, where's the second intruder?"

A shiver ran up Julie's spine. "I suppose it's too much to hope that the first gunman just got knocked out."

Chris looked at her over his shoulder, his brows raised. "You're worried about a man who tried to kill you?"

She shrugged, feeling silly. "I just don't like the idea of being responsible for someone's death."

A shuttered look came over his face. "Seems like I remember you thanking God yesterday after your husband was killed."

She jerked back, feeling his censure like a physical blow. "I never wanted Alan to die. I was thanking

God that Alan couldn't hurt me again. But I didn't mean I was glad he'd been killed."

Chris's face softened. "It's not my place to pass judgment either way. I shouldn't have said anything." He turned back to the house, intently watching for signs of any gunmen.

Julie felt sick inside that he'd thought she was grateful for Alan's death. That was an awful thing to think about someone. Yet, here he was again, protecting her.

"Why?" she blurted out before she could stop herself.

"Why what?" Again, he didn't turn around, just kept his gun trained toward the house.

"Why are you helping me if you think I'm the kind of person who would rejoice over my husband being killed?"

He sighed heavily and reached toward her. "Take my hand, Julie."

She hesitated.

"Please."

His tone was gentle, imploring. She shoved her useless empty gun into the waistband of her khaki pants and put her right hand in his left one.

He tugged her up beside him, still not taking his gaze from the dying fire and the building.

"I'm a cop," he said. "A detective. It's my nature to doubt everything, to assume the worst. It's how I stay alive. Yes, I thought you were happy that your husband was dead." He glanced at her. "I also thought you might have planned the whole thing, moving in next to a cop and arranging that confrontation when you knew I'd be home."

She gasped and tried to tug her hand out of his grasp, but he tightened his hold.

"I don't think that anymore. Okay? I saw the truth in your eyes, heard it in your voice back in the house when you answered my questions."

His thumb lightly brushed the underside of her wrist, doing crazy things to her pulse and her breathing.

"You're a victim—"

"No. I am *not* a victim."

He squeezed her hand. "You're right. You're not. You're a witness, and a strong woman. Most people I know, most men I know, would have stayed in that bathtub. They wouldn't have gotten out because they were worried the police officer protecting them might need help. And the moment they heard someone else in the house, they would have frozen or run screaming. Instead, you covered me. You kept that rifleman busy when I was focused on shooting the propane tank. I might have saved you yesterday. But you saved me today. You're one of the bravest women I know. And, trust me, my respect for you has grown exponentially this morning."

"Thank you," she whispered, her throat tight. "And I do trust you."

He smiled and faced the house. Then he stiffened

and pulled his hand from hers. "The second gunman's making a run for it. He's heading for the barn."

Julie leaned sideways, trying to see what he saw.

"Wait here!" Chris sprinted past her, arms and legs pumping as he ran toward the house. He stopped at the far corner, sweeping his gun out in front of him.

The horses let out shrill whinnies and bolted to the other side of the corral, as far from the barn as they could get. A dark figure seemed to materialize from out of nowhere, running around Chris's pickup toward the barn.

Chris dropped to his knees, aiming his pistol with both hands.

The sound of a distant siren filled the air, coming up the road.

"Yes, hurry. Please," Julie whispered, praying that help arrived soon. It was killing her watching Chris risk his life like this.

He fired off several shots. A metallic ping sounded from the truck where a bullet buried itself in the driver's-side door, narrowly missing the gunman.

The man returned fire. Chris let loose with a volley of shots. The gunman clutched his shoulder and spun around, dropping to the ground.

Chris took off, legs pumping like a champion sprinter as he ran toward the truck. Julie clutched the tree as she watched, bark cutting into her fingertips. The siren was much closer now.

The gunman rolled beneath the pickup, firing

a couple of quick shots of his own. Chris dove toward the questionable cover of the fence, bringing up his pistol again. But the gunman had rolled out the other side.

Another pickup suddenly barreled into view, gravel and dirt spitting out in a dark cloud from beneath its wheels as it raced toward the corral. Lights flashed in the grill and its shrill siren filled the air. Julie recognized the driver as one of the SWAT officers she'd met after her husband was shot—Randy Carter.

Chris jumped up, motioning in the direction where the gunman had disappeared.

Another cloud of dust billowed up as a black Dodge Charger raced from the other side of the barn where it must have been parked. It took off across the open field, bumping and weaving like a drunk between the enormous hay bales.

Julie heard Chris's shout as he waved for Randy to pursue the Charger. More sirens sounded from somewhere out front. Chris watched the truck chasing the Charger across the field. Julie could no longer see them because of the trees. When she looked back at Chris, he was jogging toward the ruins of the exploded propane tank and what was left of the rifleman's last hiding place.

Her fingers curled against the tree trunk again as she waited like he'd asked.

Two vehicles—an old black Camry and a white Ford Escape—pulled up on each side of the house, parking sideways at the far corner where the side yard and backyard met.

The drivers, a man and a woman, hopped out in full SWAT gear, both of them crouching down behind the engine blocks of their respective vehicles. They kept their long guns pointed up toward the sky in deference to Chris, but obviously they were there to support him in any way he might need.

He slowly straightened from crouching over something on the ground and motioned for both officers to join him. They rushed forward in unison, their motions well-rehearsed and sure, as if they'd practiced this type of situation hundreds of times.

After a brief consultation with Chris, the officers took off their helmets. Julie recognized them as having been at her rental home and later at the police station. She couldn't remember the man's name, but the woman, the one who'd arrived in the Escape, was Donna Waters. She'd sat beside Julie after the shooting.

And heard Julie praying her thanks.

She winced as Donna started toward her, apparently at Chris's request. Officer Waters probably thought Julie was a horrible person, as Chris had.

Straightening her shoulders, Julie pushed away from the tree to meet her halfway.

Donna was probably only a few years older than Julie, maybe twenty-eight or twenty-nine. Her blond hair was cut in a short, wavy style that flattered her heart-shaped face. They met in the side yard. Contrary to the chilly reception that Julie had expected—given the misunderstanding over her prayer after Alan's death—Donna gave her a sympathetic smile and hugged her.

"Bless your heart," the officer said when she pulled back. Genuine sympathy stared back from her blue eyes. "Not the best reception Destiny has ever given a newcomer. I'm so sorry, sweetie. How ya holding up?"

"Um, fine, I guess. Thank you."

Donna squeezed her shoulder. "I really hate to ask this. But Chris wants you to ID the body."

Julie took an instinctive step back. "The body?"

"You don't have to. It's totally okay, and understandable. But we think you might know the guy who tried to shoot you two. He was apparently facing away from the blast when Chris shot the tank. So…"

"His face wasn't burned up."

Donna nodded. "It'll just take a second. Only if you're okay with it. Chris told me to make sure you know you don't have to do this."

She swallowed the bile rising in her throat. "But he thinks, you all think, that I know the man who… the rifleman?"

"We do."

"Why?"

"It's something you'd have to see to understand." She waited, then nodded again, smiling. "It was a lot to ask, after everything you've been through. Just wait here and I'll tell them you can't—"

"I'll do it." Julie hurried past her, walking at a brisk pace. For some unfathomable reason, Chris wanted her to look at a dead man. So that's what she was going to do. And if she didn't do it fast, before she had time to think, she knew she couldn't go through with it.

Donna rushed to catch up to her. Together they approached the two men. Julie kept her gaze trained on Chris. He was watching her like a hawk, looking as if he would grab her and pull her away if she showed any signs of faltering.

She stopped a few feet in front of him, sensing more than seeing the body on the ground at her feet.

"You don't have to do this," he said.

"I know. But you want me to?"

He slowly nodded. "I do."

She drew a shaky breath. "Okay. Then I will."

The man standing beside him—Max maybe?—gave them both a surprised look. She could see him in her peripheral vision, as if he was puzzled by their exchange. Was it unusual for a witness to trust a cop the way she did Chris? Maybe, probably. But she'd been through more trials and tribulations in the past twenty-four hours with him than she'd ever been with most of the people in her life. And every single time she needed him, he was there. She did trust him, completely. And that had her so scared she was shaking inside.

She closed her eyes, gathered her courage, then did what he'd asked.

She looked down at the body.

And then she knew why he'd asked her to come over here, hoping she could identify the man who'd most recently tried to kill her. Sadly, no, she didn't recognize him. Had, in fact, never seen him before in her life. Because if she had, she'd never have forgotten him.

He could have been her twin.

Chapter Fifteen

Chris thanked the restaurant manager and closed the door to the private dining room. Several tables had been pulled together in the center of the room to accommodate Julie, the chief and the entire SWAT team minus Dillon—who was staying at the hospital with his wife.

Surprisingly, the chief was treating Chris just as if he was on active duty and had yet to gripe at him over spiriting Julie away from the station. Maybe the chief was giving him a break for surviving another close call. Or maybe he was rewarding Chris for getting Julie to really talk to them. Then again, it could just be that without Dillon the department was stretched too thin. Regardless of the reason, Chris was glad to be part of the team again.

A banquet of fried chicken, mashed potatoes, corn, lima beans and corn bread was laid out in front of them—the perfect Sunday lunch spread after a long morning at church. Or, in Chris and Julie's case, a morning spent dodging bullets and blowing up propane tanks.

He sat beside Julie, who seemed a bit stunned at the volume of food in front of them.

"Go on," Chris urged. "You haven't had anything to eat today."

She nodded and accepted a bowl of mashed potatoes from Donna, who was sitting on her other side.

Everyone was quiet as they ate, without the usual conversation or gossip they usually shared when all of them ended up at the same table—an event that was rare and usually enjoyed. But not today. Today food was just that—food, energy to get through whatever else was going to happen during this investigation.

Since Cooper's farm was a crime scene, it had been cordoned off and a dozen CSU techs and police officers were processing it for clues. Only five of those officers were Destiny police. The rest had been "borrowed" from the state police and neighboring counties, as often happened whenever there was a major crime scene.

Julie set a chicken leg on her plate and offered the platter to Chris. He murmured his thanks and put a breast and a thigh on his own plate before handing the platter across the table to the chief.

"So, the guy in the Charger got away?" Julie asked.

Randy winced beside the chief. "He got off a lucky shot and took out my left front tire. I overcorrected the resulting skid and slammed into a tree."

"I'm so sorry," Julie said. "You're okay?"

He nodded, looking pleased that she'd ask. "I'm fine. My truck needed a new paint job. Now I get it for free, courtesy of the Destiny Police Department."

Thornton frowned his displeasure at his officer, but didn't deny that the department would pick up the tab.

Chris noted that Julie played with her food more than she ate. Not that he could blame her. His own usually healthy appetite—especially when it came to fried chicken—was nearly nonexistent. There were too many questions rolling around in his head. Plus the worry that something could happen to Julie. There was zero doubt now that more than one person was after her, trying to kill her. Whatever was going on was bigger than a soon to be ex-husband wanting to settle the score.

Several minutes later, Chief Thornton pushed back his plate and wiped his hands on his napkin. That seemed to be the signal that everyone had been waiting for. They all put their forks down.

"Before anyone asks," Julie said, "I've been racking my brain about the rifleman, like you all told me to do before we left Cooper's farm. I still don't know who he is…was."

"He sure had an uncanny resemblance to you," Chris said. "Just how sure are you that he wasn't a long-lost brother?"

She rolled her eyes. "If I had a brother, I'd know about it."

"Doppelganger," Randy said, with the solemnity of a sage oracle, as if he'd just figured out the secret to life.

Julie frowned. "Doppelganger?"

"Don't," Chris warned.

"Don't what?"

"Encourage him. He's got all kinds of crazy theories. We try not to get him started."

Randy pressed a hand against his shirt, feigning hurt even as he winked at Julie. "A doppelganger is an evil twin. They say everyone has one somewhere in the world. Today you met yours."

"Evil twin?" Julie asked.

Donna shook her head. "That's not what a doppelganger is. A doppelganger is a ghost, an apparition who's the spitting image of you. Obviously, if you'd met your doppelganger it would be a woman."

Randy crossed his arms over his chest. "Then how do you explain the gunman? He looked just like Mrs. Webb. But she insists she doesn't have any long-lost brothers. So what other explanation is there?"

Chris tossed his napkin on top of his plate. "Obviously, Julie is related to the gunman somehow. The CSU guys submitted his prints. Hopefully, we'll get a hit, and get it soon. In the meantime, we need to shake the Webb family tree and see who falls out. Julie, you can help by giving us some background on your family."

"I already told you about my sister, and what happened to my parents."

The pain in her voice had him hating himself for having to ask her even more questions. But worse would be standing at her graveside while they lowered her casket. To help, he briefed everyone on what she'd already told him.

Donna took a small notebook and pen from her purse. Like the others, she was still dressed in her Sunday best. But her dark blue dress was horribly wrinkled because of the body armor she'd worn earlier. She didn't seem to mind.

She made some notes and smiled at Julie. "Can you tell me your parents' names?"

Julie looked at Chris. "This is supposed to help you figure out the gunman's identity?"

"It's a starting place, victimology," Chris said. "In order to find out why your husband tried to kill you, and who else is after you, we need to know as much as we can about your history. That includes your family, your friends, your work—everything."

She let out a long-suffering sigh. "Okay. Fine. My mom was Beatrix. My father was Giles Linwood. They were both born and raised in London, England. But their parents didn't approve of them dating. Well, mostly my mom's parents didn't approve. Mom said they had some money and thought my dad was a gold digger. After my grandfather died, my grandmother—Elizabeth—took an even harder stance against my mom and dad dating. They ended up getting married anyway. Grandmother disowned my mom and she and my dad moved to America to start a new life.

"Disowned," Donna said. "Sounds old-fashioned."

Julie shrugged. "I don't know much about my grandmother, but old-fashioned covers it. She was big on loyalty and felt my mom had turned her back on the family by marrying my father."

"Did you ever meet her?" Chris asked.

"No. I've never heard from her or any of my parents' relatives. But my mother had a necklace that was given to her by my grandmother when Mom turned eighteen. She passed it on to my sister, Naomi, on her eighteenth birthday, saying it was a family tradition and that she must promise to always keep the necklace safe. When Naomi…when Naomi died, my mom told me to take the necklace, that it was mine now."

She shook her head. "That's all I have of my English heritage, just a stupid necklace. Once my parents died, I had an estate sale, got rid of the furniture, clothes, things I figured someone else might need. I've never been much of a packrat. But I couldn't bear to let go of some things—pictures mostly, my mom's costume jewelry that she loved so much, Dad's baseball card collection. And the few things I had of Naomi's, including that necklace and her hairclips."

The earlier tortured look in her eyes faded as she smiled at the memory of her sister. "She had a fetish for the darn clips, snatched them up at flea markets and estate sales, the gaudier the better. If you pasted rhinestones or fake gems onto something to put in your hair, Naomi would drool over it. I'd forgotten about that. I put the box away for safe-keeping, but haven't looked at it even once since then. I think... looking at their things would make it too real that I'll never see my family again."

Chris was about to ask her more about her sister when the chief's phone rang. The chief apologized and stepped away from the table to take the call.

A few seconds later, Max's phone rang, too. Conversation stopped while both men took their calls. When they were done, Chris glanced back and forth between them.

"Well?" he asked. "Something about the investigation?"

The chief nodded. "Mine was. Kathy Nelson said she needs Mrs. Webb to return to Nashville in order to wrap up the loose ends of the criminal case that was pending against Mr. Webb. She's demanding that we escort her there right away." He arched a brow at Julie.

"I don't see why I need to be there. She already has my statements about Alan breaking into our home in Nashville. What happened here doesn't change the case."

"I agree," the chief said. "Which is why I told her not to hold her breath, that you'd leave if and when you were ready."

Julie blinked, looking half-horrified that he'd talk

to an ADA that way, and half-amused. "Um, thanks. I think."

Detective Max Remington leaned forward, resting his arms on the table at his seat on the end. "My call was about the case, too. The license plate check on the black Dodge Charger came through. The car is owned by a rental company. You'll never guess where it's based."

"Nashville," Chris said. "Do I get to guess who rented it?"

"You could, but I'd rather tell you. The car was rented by assistant district attorney Kathy Nelson."

Julie let out a gasp of surprise.

"She wasn't driving," the chief said. "The call I just took was from a landline in Nashville. I know because it was the ADA's receptionist who put the call through. And she told me Nelson was in court all morning, with another ADA, and they'd both just gotten back into the office. No way could she have done that and been driving through hay fields a few hours ago."

"Agreed," Chris said, still watching Max. "But I don't think the car was rented for her use. The Charger was rented for one of her assistants, wasn't it, Max?"

"Yep. The winning answer is Brian Henson. A second car, also black, this one a Chevy Camaro, was rented by Nelson for her other assistant, Jonathan Bolton."

"I don't remember seeing a Charger or a Camaro

parked in the police when they were at the station," Chris said. "All I saw was Nelson's silver Mercedes. Why would she rent cars for her assistants—separate cars—but all three of them arrive together at the station?"

The chief stood and pulled out his phone again. "You don't have to say it. I'm calling Nelson back right now to ask about her assistants and her rental-car habits. This is getting really weird is all I have to say." He headed to the other side of the dining room.

"I don't understand," Julie said. "We're saying that Kathy's employee, Henson, tried to kill us this morning? And that because Kathy drove both of her administrative assistants to the police station for my interview, that she was—what—planning the attack and didn't want us to know what cars her men drove? That doesn't make any sense. She's an assistant district attorney. An old college friend. What would she have to gain by having me killed?"

"I'm not sure we're ready to make all of those leaps in logic, yet," Chris said. "We're just gathering facts. But if we do assume that Nelson is behind the attempt on your life this morning, then it makes sense to also assume that she could have been working with Alan and that together they may have orchestrated both times that he attacked you."

She pressed her hand against her throat. "I don't... I don't see how that's possible. She and Alan couldn't stand each other."

Chris leaned forward. "You sure about that? For

all you know, Kathy and Alan may have been far more than friends in college and hid it from you. Maybe they already knew each other when you and her supposedly first met him."

Julie shook her head. "No. No, that can't be. I'm telling you, they really didn't get along in college. Besides, even if I were wrong—which I'm not—if they were interested in each other, all they had to do was date and leave me as the third wheel. We're the same age. We were all struggling college students, with nothing to gain or lose by becoming friends or hiding any attractions. What would be the point? If Kathy liked Alan, and vice versa, they'd have become an item instead of Alan and me." She spread her hands out in front of her. "On top of that, if Kathy liked Alan, it would have been in her best interest to let him know back then, not hide it and encourage me in my relationship with him, which is what she did."

"She encouraged you to date him?" Chris asked.

"Basically. I mean it wasn't like she pushed me toward him. But she seemed happy for me and made sure that I knew she didn't mind when I did essentially choose my boyfriend over spending time with her."

"You said it would have been in her best interest to date Alan," Chris continued. "Why?"

"Money, of course. He wasn't exactly flush in college, but he wasn't hurting either. Everyone knew he was the heir to Webb Enterprises, his father's import-export business, and that he was expected to take the reins of the company one day. Whoever ended up marrying Alan would have come into a lot of money. If this is about Kathy and Alan being some kind of partners, they would have become partners in college and gotten married. I had nothing to offer anyone. There was no financial benefit for Alan marrying me."

"I'm not so sure that's true," Max said from the end of the table, just as the chief resumed his seat.

The chief waved toward him. "I got some silly runaround answer from Nelson about her men wanting to explore the countryside, thus the rental of two cars. And she'd driven them to the station because they were all at the hotel together and it made sense to share a ride to Mrs. Webb's witness interview." He rolled his eyes.

"I'm still not buying it," the chief continued. "Especially since they didn't end up staying overnight at the hotel. Naturally, her response to my question about that was that they changed their minds after Julie left the interview. But unless the city of Nashville has money to burn in their budget, I don't see them reimbursing an ADA for renting her admin assistants cars." He waved at Max again. "Go on. You were about to say something else you found out?"

Max nodded. "Mrs. Webb, you mentioned your mother's family had some money. Any idea how much?"

Julie shook her head. "My mom didn't talk about her family very often. I got the impression they lived comfortably, but not anything crazy. It's not like they were millionaires, or however many pounds sterling it takes to make someone rich." She smiled, but Max remained stoic.

"You didn't mention your mother's maiden name earlier," Max said.

"Abbott, why?"

He nodded, as if that was what he'd expected. "Your grandmother was Elizabeth Victoria Abbott, correct?" Max asked.

Julie frowned. "Yes, that's right. Is there a point here somewhere?"

"Your grandmother's late husband was Edward. They were from old money and built that inheritance into an extremely lucrative corporation they simply named Victoria and Edward. Your grandfather died many years ago. But your grandmother is still alive and thriving. She's the CEO. And you're right that she's not worth millions. Her net worth is in the billions. About two-point-six billion, to be exact."

The room went silent.

Julie's mouth dropped open.

"There's one other piece of information I got from that call," Max said, shifting his glance to Chris and then the chief. "The fingerprint search on our dead rifleman got a match based on a passport-database search." He looked back at Julie. "His name was Harry Abbott."

Chapter Sixteen

Julie yanked the comb through her wet hair, wincing when it caught on a tangle. She freed the comb and tossed it into the duffel bag that Donna had gotten for her from the rental house. The chief had been nice enough to let Julie take a shower in the bathroom attached to his office here at the police station. This luxury had surprised her and elicited a few snickers from the SWAT team.

Julie braced her hands on the countertop and stared into the mirror above the sink, thinking about what she'd learned during lunch. Her mom had painted Julie's grandmother as being ancient, in poor health. Julie had always assumed the woman had passed away by now. But now she knew her grandmother was alive and well, and at the helm of a multibillion-pound enterprise.

Not that it made any difference. Julie would have loved to have a grandmother, regardless of her grandmother's financial situation. She longed for someone to help fill the holes in her heart left by the loss of her family. But obviously that sentiment wasn't returned. If Elizabeth Abbott had really loved her only daughter, she'd have done something over the years to reach out to her. And she'd have discovered she had two granddaughters to love, as well. But she never had. Which told Julie that her mother was right all along, and that she'd made the right choice in fleeing across the pond when she was just a girl herself.

Julie shoved her hair back from her eyes, straightened the bathroom, then grabbed the duffel and headed into the chief's office. She stopped short when she saw Chris writing on a whiteboard hanging on the wall opposite the desk.

He turned and smiled a greeting. Then his smile died as he looked at her. "Julie? What's wrong?"

She glanced at the closed door, relieved that no one else was in the office right now. She sat in one of the guest chairs in front of the chief's desk.

"I'm not normally a whiner. But I'm beginning to seriously dislike my grandmother even though I've never met her. I can't get past the fact that she's as rich as Midas but could never forgive her daughter and provide the help that Naomi needed, the help my parents could never afford. If she had, maybe Naomi would still be alive."

Chris crossed the room and crouched in front of her chair, taking her hands in his. "Are you saying your grandmother contacted your mother? That she knew she had granddaughters, and didn't do anything to intercede when your sister got sick?"

She clung to his hands, to the strength and support he offered, grateful to have one person she felt comfortable with, one person she could lean on right now.

"No. But I just can't see my loving, wonderful mother not reaching out to *her* mother to save her dying child. If there was anything humanly possible that could be done to save Naomi, my mom would have done it. So I have to believe that she did contact my grandmother, told her the situation and asked for her help."

Julie shook her head, tears tracking down her cheeks. "No help came. My grandmother chose her feud over trying to save the life of her eldest granddaughter. How can I ever forgive that?"

He pulled her into his arms and held her tight. Embarrassed to be crying on him again, she tried to think of something else—anything else—to stop her tears. But blanking all her troubles from her mind left far too much room to think about how good his arms felt around her.

The last time she and her husband had held each other like this had been too long ago to remember. That had to be why she felt so drawn to this man. She was lonely, starved for affection, desperate for someone who seemed to care what happened to her. But, really, who wouldn't be drawn to him?

His strong arms felt wonderful around her. His chest was the perfect pillow for her cheek. And he smelled so darn good. But of course there was so much more to him than the physical. He was brave, protective, loyal—the qualities that meant the most to Julie, probably because those were the qualities of a tight-knit family. And family meant everything to her. Which was why losing hers had been so devastating.

For just a moment, she allowed herself the fantasy of pretending that Chris was her family, that he was hers to hold and to keep and treasure. It was a delightful fantasy, and one that would be over far too soon. Because even if he felt the same draw, the same attraction—heart, soul and mind—to her that she felt to him, what kind of a future could there ever be for a relationship between so very different people?

She'd seen how close he was to his SWAT team, how they acted like their own little family. He could never give up something like that, give up the friends he was loyal to and cared about. And she wouldn't want him to. But she couldn't see herself in a small town like this for the rest of her life. Her work meant far too much to her, and it relied on charity, the kinds of donations she could only get by working in a large city with affluent pools of people to draw upon—a city like Nashville. Moving here, to Destiny, permanently, would mean giving up on finding cures that would help so many families like hers. That was something she just couldn't do.

Inhaling deeply, she selfishly enjoyed another tantalizing breath warmed by Chris's skin, perfumed by his masculine scent. Then she pushed herself back to sitting, forcing him to drop his arms.

He studied her intently, his dark eyes boring into hers. "You do know that I'm going to protect you, right? You seem…scared, or maybe worried."

Unable to stop herself, she caressed his face. Her heart nearly stopped when he rubbed his cheek against her hand. Oh, how she wished her life were different, that she had met this man in another place, another time.

He smiled, a warm, gentle smile she felt all the way to her toes.

"Everything's going to be okay, Julie," he said. "We'll figure this out. Together."

"Thank you," she whispered. Her gaze dropped to his lips, and she automatically leaned toward him. Her hands went to his shirt, smoothing the fabric.

A shudder went through him and she looked up. The open hunger on his face made her breath catch. And then he was leaning toward her, slowly, giving her every chance to stop him, to pull away, to say no.

She didn't want to say no.

She wanted his lips on hers, his arms around her, wanted to feel her breasts crushing against the hard planes of his chest. She wanted this. She wanted him, needed him.

His breath warmed her as he kissed first one cheek, then the other, before lowering his lips to hers.

Heaven. She'd died and gone to heaven, and it was far better than she'd ever thought it could be. His mouth moved against hers, softly, gently, a warm caress that made her feel cherished, wanted, needed, the way that she needed him. The kiss was so beautiful it made her want to cry all over again, this time with joy. And then the kiss changed.

Gone was the gentle lover. The hunger she'd seen on his face, in his eyes, she now felt in his touch, in the way his arms crushed her against him, the way his lips slanted across hers. His tongue swept inside her mouth, a hot, wild mating, urgent and demanding. Her pulse rushed in her ears, her heart beating against her ribs as she slid her arms up around his neck.

He groaned deep in his throat and lifted her out of the chair, turning with her in his arms and never taking his lips from hers. He pressed her back against the whiteboard. She lifted her legs, wrapping them around his waist. The kiss was hot, ravenous, full of need and longing for more, so much more.

She pulled her arms down to his shirt and began working the top button, then the next. When she reached the third, she slid her hands inside his shirt, reveling in the feel of his hot skin against hers. And just like that, they both broke the kiss, staring in shock at each other.

"Oh, my," she breathed. "I think I was about to tear your clothes off."

"I was about to help." He chuckled and pressed his forehead against hers. He drew a ragged breath before pulling back and smiling down at her. "Where did that come from?"

She shook her head. "I have no idea. But it probably happens to you all the time."

His eyes widened. "Why would you say that?"

She slid her arms up behind his neck, then realized what she was doing and forced them down. He eased back and helped her stand, keeping his hands on her shoulders as if she needed steadying—which she definitely did.

"Why did you say it happens all the time to me?" he repeated.

She rolled her eyes and waved toward the three undone buttons on his shirt. "Because of…that. You're gorgeous. And charming. And smart. And a dozen other things. Women probably throw themselves at you so much you have to fight them off."

Her cheeks grew hot under his incredulous stare. "What?" she demanded, feeling extremely self-conscious.

"Have you seen yourself in a mirror lately, Julie? You can't tell me that you didn't notice how Max and the others kept looking at you during lunch. You're beautiful."

It was her turn to stare at him with an incredulous expression. "Now that I think about it, I remember seeing you bump your head after the propane tank exploded. Isn't that right? Now it all makes sense."

He laughed and buttoned up his shirt, much to her sorrow. And then she laughed, too, because this was the lightest she'd felt in months. Which made no sense at all considering that someone was trying to kill her.

That thought helped sober her up and, unfortunately, killed the good mood Chris had managed to put her in. Her gaze fell to the duffel bag, forgotten on the floor, and just like that all of the horrible things that had been happening since that night that Alan had broken into their Nashville home flooded back.

A gentle touch beneath her chin had her looking up into Chris's eyes. He gave her a sad smile. "You're back to worrying again, I see. I wish there was something that I could do to convince you it's all going to work out."

"Me, too." She pointed at the whiteboard. "What is all of that?"

He picked up a pen and piece of paper from on top of the desk and held them out to her. "I'll tell you in a minute. First, though. I'd like your written permission to search your home in Nashville and to open the safe. The chief will notarize the document. We'll need the house keys. And we'll use your written permission to get a locksmith to open the safe."

She took the paper, skimmed the two paragraphs of legalize. "How did you know the address?" She set the paper on the desk to sign it, then grabbed her purse from another corner of the desk.

"The night the chief interviewed you, the paperwork you filled out gave your basic info, including addresses. You don't remember?"

She worked the required key off her key ring as

she shook her head. "Not really. Everything that night is kind of a blur at this point. And I'd prefer to keep it that way."

She set the house key on top of the form she'd signed and tossed the rest of her keys into her purse. "Do I need to sign anything else?"

"Not at the moment. I'll get one of our guys working on this right away." He picked up the key and paper and strode out of the office.

Julie crossed to the whiteboard, trying to make sense of what Chris had written on it. There were several columns, in varying colors, with bullets beneath each column.

"I'm a list maker," he announced as he came back into the office and shut the door. "If I can make a list out of something, it organizes my thoughts, helps me form a big picture and then put all the pieces together."

She smiled. "I'm a list maker, too. What does all of this mean?"

He walked her through it, and she noted how he'd used different colored markers for different categories. Suspects were written in green.

Kathy Nelson.
Brian Henson.
Jonathan Bolton.
Alan Webb—Deceased.
Harry Abbott—Deceased.

She rubbed her hands up and down her arms. "I thought Kathy had an alibi for when we were at Cooper's farm?"

"She does. But if she put out the hit, she's just as guilty. Even without evidence, that seems like the simplest explanation for everything. And usually the most straightforward explanation is the right one. I also don't believe in coincidences. When looking at this as a whole, Kathy and Alan working together against you is the basic premise that makes the most sense. But we have to figure out what they were after, which leads me to my next column."

He wrote on the board—Motive. And beneath that he created another list.

Love.
Money.
Revenge.
Hatred.
Hide something.

He turned around. "Every case I've ever worked fell into one of these categories, often more than one. At the heart of every murder, one of these overrides all else and drives the killer. Looking at Alan first, we know that he wanted to kill you. But it seems like he was also after something else—perhaps this key that you mentioned. So which of the motivations seems to make sense as to why he did what he did?"

She cocked her head, studying the list, thinking

about how her relationship with Alan had started, how it had been so warm and loving in college, and then how it had changed shortly after they got married. She grew still, trying to figure out what, if anything, that might mean.

"What is it?" Chris asked. "You've thought of something."

"You said you don't believe in coincidences. And yet Alan just happened to appear the moment when I needed him the most. Just a few months after I lost my family, and my support system, when I was at rock bottom, he was there. Strong, understanding, helping me work through my grief. Given everything else, that just feels...wrong."

Chris slowly lowered the dry-erase marker that he was holding. "Tell me how your family died again. Don't leave anything out."

She frowned. "I don't see how that—"

"Humor me."

She shrugged. "Okay. Naomi got sick—"

"And the doctors couldn't figure out what was wrong with her."

"Right."

"Why not?"

"Excuse me?"

He set the marker onto the ledge. "Doctors used to have to rely on their memories, or look up symptoms in some thick medical tome to try to figure out what illness or disease matched them. Nowadays, they can plug symptoms into any number of online tools and get a list of possible causes. Doesn't it seem strange that they couldn't do that in your sister's case?"

She shook her head, uncomfortable with where the conversation seemed to be heading. "It's not strange. That's the thing about orphan diseases. They don't come up in internet searches if they're so rare that no one has input any information about them into a computer. The doctors said she must have had an orphan disease."

"But they couldn't give it a name?"

"No, they couldn't."

"Again, why not?"

She spread her hands in a helpless gesture. "I suppose because her symptoms kept changing. And each symptom came on so suddenly. Really, by the time my parents realized how seriously ill she was, and that she wasn't getting better, she only had a few weeks left. She died four months after the first day she got sick. But my parents had only started hounding the doctors about six or eight weeks before that. I think that's why it hit them so hard. They felt guilty for not seeking help sooner."

"I can totally see that, a parent thinking their child had a cold or virus, expecting it to go away on its own. It would be particularly difficult to realize how bad it was if the symptoms changed."

"Exactly. That's why my dad spiraled into a deep depression after her death. He felt he should have done more." She twisted her hands together in her lap. "We all felt we should have done more."

She braced herself for his sympathy, not wanting him to feel sorry for her. But, as if sensing how she felt, he gave her one quick empathetic look before grabbing a dry-erase pen and moving to the right side of the board. He wrote "Naomi" and "Symptoms" on top of a new column.

"Tell me her symptoms, in the exact order in which they appeared, and tell me how long they lasted."

"I don't understand. Why do you want me to re-live that pain again?"

His jaw tightened. "I don't want to hurt you, Julie. But more importantly, I want to save your life. If that means I have to cause you a little pain to do it, then I will."

Had she really thought of this man as her fantasy-hero a few minutes ago? Her perfect man? Because right now, she just wanted to walk out of this office and turn her back on the wounds he was opening inside her.

"Julie, you told me that you trust me. Was that a lie?"

His gentle, soothing voice wrapped around her heart like velvet. "No," she finally said. "That wasn't a lie. I do trust you."

"Then work with me on this. Tell me Naomi's symptoms. What was the first thing you or your parents noticed?"

She worked with him for over half an hour on the list. Each time she thought they were done, he'd ask another question, force her to delve deeper into her memory, try to associate each appearance or disappearance of a symptom with some event in her life to help her make sure she had it right.

Finally, he stepped back from the board, taking it all in. He seemed deep in thought. And when he turned around, Julie could have sworn she saw a flash of anger in his eyes. But the emotion was quickly masked with one of his kind, gentle smiles. He took her hands in his and led her to the door.

He pulled it open, and she looked up at him in confusion. "You want me to leave?"

He waved at Donna, who was sitting at one of the desks, typing on her computer. She hurried over, raising a brow in question.

"Donna, can you show Julie the kitchenette and get her something to drink? I need to make a phone call."

Donna smiled and put an arm around Julie's shoulders. "No problem. Come on, sweetie. Calories don't count during murder investigations. And thanks to Ashley, Dillon's wife, we've always got all kinds of goodies over here. I'll pull a batch of her banana nut muffins out of the freezer and heat them up. They're amazing."

She led Julie to what Chris had called a kitchenette but that was really just a long counter against the wall to the right of the chief's office door and to the left of the main door into the station. It was loaded with cookies and all kinds of other baked goods, with a coffeemaker on one end and both a small refrigerator and a freezer underneath the counter on the other.

"Soda, coffee or water?" Donna asked. "Pick your poison."

"Um, soda, I guess. Something with a lot of caffeine. Thanks."

"You got it." Donna opened the refrigerator.

Julie looked toward the chief's office, but Chris had already closed the door.

"SORRY TO BUG you again, Dillon. But this is really important," Chris said into the phone as he stared at the white board. Just thinking about what he now believed to be true had him wanting to go to the morgue and kill Alan Webb all over again

"Not a problem," Dillon whispered. "Give me a second."

Chris heard the sound of muted footsteps, as if Dillon was trying not to make any noise. A moment later, a click. "Okay. I'm out of Ashley's room. This is the first real sleep she's had since we got here and I didn't want to disturb her."

"Does that mean what I think it means?"

"We think this scary episode is over now, yes. She hasn't had any contractions in quite a while. Go ahead. Tell me what you've got."

"I'm asking you to go way back to your college days, to all those fancy medical classes you took when you wanted to be a large-animal vet."

"I'll pay you back for calling me old the next time

I see you, especially since we're the same age. What classes specifically are you talking about?"

"Did you take any botany classes?"

"Of course. I needed to know what kinds of plants were poisonous and recognize the symptoms in case of accidental ingestion by an animal. Why?"

"That's what I figured. I've got a list of symptoms for you, and then I want you to tell me what comes to mind."

There was a long pause before Dillon spoke. "Shouldn't you be calling an actual botanist or doctor about this?"

"I will, or I'll have one of the guys follow up. But I figured this would be faster and you could at least tell me if what I'm thinking is crazy."

"All right. I've got my pen and notebook out. Go."

It didn't take long. The anger that had been building inside Chris was now ready to explode.

"What was this Alan Webb guy's major in college?" Dillon asked.

"Botany."

"You know what you need to do."

"Yeah. I need to exhume Naomi's body."

Chapter Seventeen

Julie was backed into a corner, literally—the one in the chief's office between the window and the door to the bathroom. It was the farthest away she could get from everyone else in the office, because they'd all lost their ever-loving minds.

She shook her head, raking the chief, Max and Chris with her glare. She'd have glared at the very nice Donna, too, and even Randy or Colby, except that they were in the squad room handling other cases that had come in.

"I won't do it," she repeated. "Naomi's gone. Digging up her body won't change that." She looked at Chris. "I can't believe you would ask me to do this."

"Did you understand what I explained about the plants? How someone can extract solanine, glycoalkaloids, arsenic—"

"Oh, I understand just fine. What you're saying is your police buddy Dillon studied plants in vet school, even though he never became a vet. And based on a short phone call and a list of symptoms I may very well remember wrong you two have come up with a crazy theory that my botany-major husband poisoned my sister. You think he switched up the plants he used so he could confuse the doctors. One set of symptoms would go away, a new set would begin, all so he could make it look like a natural death when there wasn't anything natural about it at all. Did I get that right, Chris? Did I explain your theory correctly?"

Tears, again the blasted tears, were running down her face. But this time they weren't tears of grief or fear. They were tears of anger.

"Did I get it right?" she demanded.

Chris slowly nodded. "Except for the part about this all being a crazy theory. I had Max confirm everything by calling a real botanist. We're not wrong about any of this, Julie. The botanist told us exactly how he could reproduce the same symptoms with plants that are easily available."

"Good for you. You get a gold star. Now, if you're through trying to rip my heart out, I'm leaving." She shoved away from the wall and strode toward the door.

Chris glanced at his boss, then moved in front of Julie, blocking her way.

"Move," she said.

"Not until you hear us out."

"I've heard all I want to hear and then some. I don't want to hear any more." She swiped at the tears. Dang it. Why couldn't she stop crying?

"Julie, please. We need to talk through this. I believe Alan poisoned your sister. If we can exhume—"

"No. I told you, no. I'm not changing my mind. And what you're saying doesn't make sense anyway. Alan never even met my sister. I didn't meet him until two months after my parents died, three months after Naomi died."

"I know." His voice was ridiculously calm. He motioned to Max. "Do you have that printout handy?"

Max pulled a sheet of paper out of his suit jacket pocket and handed it to Chris.

Julie tried to grab the doorknob, but Chris planted a foot to his left, again blocking her. He opened the paper and started to read what amounted to a short bio about Alan.

Julie shook her head, her hands fisted at her sides. "Some investigators you people are. You've got his birthdate wrong. He wasn't two years older than me. He and I were the same age."

"Max," Chris said in that infuriatingly calm, soothing voice. "Where did you get Alan's birthdate?"

A look of sympathy crossed Max's face as he answered. "Mrs. Webb, I know your husband told you he was your age. But it was a ruse so he could enroll in the same classes as you without raising red flags. Even more damning, the classes he took at your college were all audited, meaning they weren't graded and didn't apply toward a degree. That's because he'd already graduated. He already had his degree from another school. That's the real reason he told you he was dropping out. He couldn't pretend to be getting a degree when you graduated. Dropping out was how he covered up that he was never a degree-seeking student at your school."

She shook her head. "No." But her voice was barely above a whisper. Panic was closing her throat.

"In addition to his school records, which had his correct birthdate, I pulled his birth certificate and cross-referenced his information in the social-security database. And if that's still not enough proof, I had a librarian pull a copy of his high-school yearbook. He graduated high school two years before you did."

He pulled another piece of paper from his jacket and handed it to Chris. "Even more importantly, I tracked down one of your sister's friends from college. That's her written statement in response to my questions. I texted her a picture of Alan off the internet from when he attended a ribbon-cutting ceremony at one of the offices for his father's company."

Chris held the paper up for Julie to see. She refused to look at it.

"The friend remembered Alan, said he went to a lot of the same bars that she and Naomi went to during Naomi's senior year, just two months before she got sick. Naomi couldn't stand Alan. He kept hitting on her and wouldn't take no for an answer. A month after she first met him, she filed a complaint against him with the local police."

"But she never...she never told me about him," Julie whispered.

He shrugged. "Maybe she didn't want to worry her family and figured filing the police report would end the problem."

With that, Max pulled another piece of paper out and handed it to Chris.

"It's the arrest report," Chris said.

The room went silent as they all waited. She stared at Max and slowly took the paper from Chris. The paper rattled because her hands were shaking so much. It was a brief report, printed on the police department's letterhead, with details like the date and the name of the officer who'd taken the statement, a statement signed by Naomi Linwood, their father's last name, Julie's maiden name.

There, at the end of the report, highlighted in yellow, was the name of the man who'd been essentially stalking Julie's sister—Alan Blackwood Webb. Exactly one month after the complaint was issued, Naomi called their mother to tell her she couldn't come home for a planned family dinner because she had an upset stomach and had thrown up three times. Four months later, Naomi was dead. And when Julie met Alan Blackwood Webb three months after that, he'd told her how sorry he was that he'd never had the pleasure of meeting her sister or her parents.

Julie lowered the piece of paper. A low buzz started in her ears.

"My father," she said, her throat so tight she could

hardly talk, "killed himself, shot himself, shortly after Naomi…died. The funny thing is, he was always so vocal against guns. He didn't even own one. But no one questioned that. We were all too grief stricken. The police assumed he'd bought it off the street. There really wasn't much of an investigation."

"Julie." Chris reached for her, but she shoved his hand away.

"Now, my mother," she continued, "was devastated when my daddy died. She'd handled Naomi's death like a soldier. But Daddy—my mom just couldn't take losing him. Couldn't sleep. Got a prescription for sleeping pills. They say she drank down the whole bottle of pills with a glass of wine."

She choked on the last word, had to cough to clear her throat. "Most people would assume the woman in a household is the wine drinker, and that the beer in the refrigerator is for the man of the house. But my mama…" Julie shook her head. "My mama was the beer drinker. I always thought it was odd that she chose to end her life drinking something she didn't even like."

She looked up at Chris through a wall of tears she could no longer stop. "He killed them. All of them. And I never even asked any questions. I accepted their deaths like everyone else. And then I married their killer."

The room began to spin around her. The buzzing got louder and louder until it was all she could hear.

Until she couldn't.

CHRIS SWORE AND caught Julie's crumpled form in his arms.

"She's passed out. Get Dr. Brookes," the chief ordered, waving at Max.

"No," Chris said, settling her higher against his chest. "She doesn't need a doctor poking at her. She needs rest, and peace and quiet. Everything about her life has come into question and she needs time to process it. Max, shove her purse into that duffel and take it out to my truck, will you?"

"You got it." Max hurried to do what he'd asked, leaving the office door open behind him.

Chris followed him out.

"Hold it," the chief ordered behind him. "You can't just walk out of here with the witness. Again."

Chris ignored the surprised look on everyone's face as he strode through the squad room. Max waited at the door, holding it open.

The chief stubbornly followed Chris into the parking lot and rushed to get in front of him when Chris stopped at his truck.

"Detective Downing, I'm ordering you to stand down. Take Mrs. Webb back into the station."

"Max, mind getting the door, please?" Chris asked.

Max seemed to be struggling to hide his grin as he held the passenger door open.

Chris settled Julie inside and fastened her seat belt before shutting the door.

"Detective," the chief barked, his face turning red.

Chris stepped around him and climbed into the driver's seat.

The chief stood in the open doorway. "If you do this, you're as good as resigning."

Chris hesitated and glanced at Julie's tear-streaked face. Somehow, in a ridiculously short amount of time, he'd gone from suspecting her of being a murderess to respecting and admiring her more than any woman he'd ever met. He'd seen her fight when others would have given up. And now, without meaning to, he'd finally ground her down to the point that she'd shut down just to survive. Taking her to a doctor or leaving her at the station to be confronted with the facts and interviewed yet again wasn't the way to heal her, to make her better. She needed to get away from the trauma she faced at every turn. And he was going to make sure she got exactly what she needed and deserved.

He turned back toward the chief. "Move."

The chief's face turned so red it looked as if he might have a stroke. Instead of moving out of the way, he called Chris every curse word that Chris had ever heard. And then he reached for his gun.

Max rushed forward. "Hey, hey, chief. Let's not get carried away."

"Shut up, Officer Remington." The chief glared at Max before looking back at Chris. "Here, take it. Yours is still locked up in evidence." He reached in his back pocket and took out a magazine, then slapped that in Chris's palm, along with the gun.

"Chief?" Chris wasn't sure what to say. And he didn't bother telling his boss he had other guns in the truck. He had a feeling that wouldn't go over well in the chief's current mood.

"That's all the ammo I got with me," the chief continued. "It's enough to keep the rattlers and bears away if you're heading up into the mountains, which is what I'd do in your situation. But if you run into any other kind of trouble, you call me. Hell, you call anyway. I want regular reports until we get all of this sorted out. You hear me, son?"

Chris was so surprised by the chief's gesture that he didn't have the heart to tell him that in addition to the weapons in his truck, he'd had Donna and Max both load up the duffel with plenty of ammo along with the clothing they'd gotten from Julie's and Chris's houses. At the time he'd assumed they'd end up in a hotel, perhaps one town over. But, as hot as this case was getting, the mountains sounded like a far better plan.

"Yes, sir," he finally said. "Thank you, Chief."

"For what? When the ADA calls asking where Mrs. Webb is, I don't know nothing. You can't thank me if I didn't do anything. You got me?"

"Yes, sir. I got you." He glanced at Max. "Keep working those angles we talked about. I'll call you later."

Max grinned. "You and Dillon always were the favorites. I'd be out on my ass if I pulled a stunt like this."

"You may still be if you don't get back in that station and follow up on those leads." The chief glared at both of them before whirling around and stalking back toward the front doors.

"Stay off the main roads as much as possible when you head out of here," Max warned. "I heard Alan Webb's family is hot over his death and might pay us a visit soon."

"When did you hear that?"

"A few minutes ago. One of my contacts warned me."

"You sure have a lot of contacts. Maybe we need to share some of them sometime."

"Nope. They're all mine." He gave Chris a jaunty salute and closed the door.

Chris checked Julie once more, then backed out of the space and took off down the road toward one of the lower peaks in the Smoky mountain range. There was a hunting cabin he and Dillon used up there during deer season. It was the perfect spot to let Julie process everything. And it also had a satellite dish, which meant that Chris could continue helping with the investigation, plus keep a tab on the efforts to locate the driver of that Charger, Brian Henson.

Chapter Eighteen

Julie rolled over in the soft bed, sighing at the fresh, clean smell of the sheets. The bed was ridiculously comfortable. The pillows fluffy, down filled. Wait, her down-filled pillows were still in boxes. Weren't they?

She gasped and bolted upright in bed. Clutching the covers to her chest, she scanned the room. A lamp was on beside the bed, casting a soft yellow glow. The walls were polished, a honey gold, and the floor beside the bed was knotty pine. Other than the lamp, the nightstand it sat on and the bed, there was nothing else. Not even a chest or dresser. None of it looked familiar. So where was she? And how had she gotten here?

"Don't panic. You're safe."

She let out a squeak of surprise, then flushed at the embarrassing sound when she recognized Chris standing in the doorway.

"Are we back at Harmony Haven?" she asked. "I don't recognize the bedroom."

"I wanted you to have some rest, some peace and quiet. So I drove us to a cabin in the mountains."

He waved his hand to encompass the room. "The rest of the place is a bit more modern, not quite this rustic. But this is the only bedroom on the first floor and I wanted you close by so I'd hear you if you woke up in a panic. You were pretty much out of it. I wasn't sure how much you'd remember of the drive up here."

She didn't remember any of it.

She blew out a long breath and shoved her hair back. A quick look down confirmed that she was still dressed in the white blouse and khaki pants that she'd been in after her shower in Chief Thornton's office. Chris must have taken her here after leaving the police station. So why couldn't she remember any of that?

All of the memories of the last confrontation in the chief's office suddenly flooded back. She squeezed her eyes shut, fighting down the panic she'd felt earlier.

He killed them.

Alan, her husband, had killed her family.

And then he'd built a life—with her.

"It gets better."

Her eyes flew open. He'd stepped beside the bed, still dressed in the jeans and casual shirt he'd changed into after his shower. The words he'd just said sat like stones in her stomach.

"What do you mean, it gets better? Your wife murdered your family, too?"

He winced, making her regret her sarcasm. She drew a deep breath, trying to calm down.

"Not exactly," he said. "I've never been married. I do know what it's like to lose someone you love. But what you're going through right now is way worse than anything I've been through. I shouldn't have said that. Sorry, I really am."

He turned as if to leave.

"No, wait. Please."

He gave her a questioning look.

She shifted in the bed, making room beside her. "Tell me about whoever you loved, and lost. Maybe... maybe it will help. Both of us."

He slowly sat down, facing her. "I've never talked about it with anyone else."

"Never?"

"No. I couldn't. I was too busy trying to be there for my best friend, to help him face his own grief. Announcing that the love of my life had just been killed in a car accident—when I'd never even told him about her—wouldn't have helped him. So I kept it inside. As the years went by, it got easier to just never talk about it."

"Your best friend? Isn't Dillon your best friend?"

"Yes."

"Then his grief—it was for the woman he named his farm after, his sister?"

"One and the same."

"That's the woman you loved and lost?"

He chuckled. "I loved Harmony, but not romantically. She was still a kid when she died, six years younger than Dillon and me." His smile faded. "But, yes, Harmony died back home, in Destiny, when Dillon and I were both away at college—separate colleges. The woman I loved, Sherry, was killed a week before Harmony. I stayed for Sherry's funeral, and to pull myself together enough to come home and tell my family and friends about her. Only, once I got here, I found out about Harmony. And Dillon was already home, and devastated."

He shook his head. "If I'd told him my own sorry tale he'd have tried to be there for me. It wouldn't have been right. I'd only been in love with Sherry for a few months. Dillon had lost his baby sister, a whole lifetime of memories. It wasn't the same."

Her heart ached for the loss Chris had suffered and for how he'd lived with it all of these years, keeping it inside. She reached for his hand and clasped it in both of hers.

"I'm so sorry, Chris. You shouldn't have had to bear that pain alone."

Slowly, ever so slowly, he leaned in toward her and placed the softest, sweetest kiss against her lips before pulling back.

"And you shouldn't have to bear your pain alone. That's why I brought you here, Julie. You've lost so much. Suffered an enormous amount of trauma, found out devastating secrets, all in a very short amount of time. I want you to know that you're safe here and I won't badger you with any more questions. We'll stay on the mountain until you're ready to come down. And in the meantime, my teammates will figure the rest of it out. We…they…will find out who's after you. And they'll stop him. I can't take away the pain you feel about what we believe happened to your family. But I can take away some of the stress, or at least try. Do you need anything? Are you hungry?"

"What I need right now is to feel normal. I don't want to talk about the case or my past or any of this. Just…talk to me, for a few minutes. About something, anything, other than the investigation."

He cocked his head, a half smile playing around his lips. "Where did you grow up? Nashville?"

She nodded.

"Ever been to the Smoky Mountains before?"

"Hasn't everybody? I've ridden on the three-story go-kart tracks in Pigeon Forge, seen Dolly Parton perform in Dollywood, gone to the stores in downtown Gatlinburg."

He grinned. "Typical tourist. You think you've seen everything, when you haven't seen anything." He stood. "Come on."

She flipped the covers back and took his hand.

He tugged her through an archway that she had assumed led to a closet. Then he unlocked and opened a door at the end. She could see blue sky and the dark green leaves of towering trees beyond.

"Wait, my shoes—"

"You don't need them."

"Easy for you to say when you're wearing shoes."

He pulled her through the doorway onto a balcony. She barely noticed the door closing behind them. Her mouth dropped open as she stared at the incredible beauty that stretched as far as she could see. Tall green pine and oak trees framed the vista to the left and the right, but directly below them the mountain steeply dropped away. A deep green valley stretched out below, and beyond that, going on for miles and miles were the blue-gray silhouettes of the Great Smoky Mountains. Little puffs of white mist rose in dozens of places, as if someone was making smoke signals. All of it combined to create a soft, beautiful haze of color and "smoke." It was as if an artist had painted the mountains, then softened everything with a light color wash.

"It's beautiful," she said. "I can't believe I've never come up into the mountains before, not like this."

"The best places in the Smokies are the ones the tourists don't know about, the little turnoffs that lead deep into the forest. There are hundreds of waterfalls all through the mountains, pristine, looking as if no one has touched them or even seen them for thousands of years. It's all unspoiled beauty. Paradise."

He leaned past her, pointing down toward the valley below. "Look," he whispered, "to the right, just coming out of the tree line."

She watched in awe as a group of three deer emerged from the forest, a doe with two fawns. The mother sniffed the air, her large ears flicking back and forth as she scanned for signs of danger. Her young pranced around her on wobbly legs, oblivious to how hard their mother worked to keep them safe. A yellow butterfly rose and dipped around them, much to the delight of the fawns, who scampered after it.

"They're so…innocent…and happy. They're gorgeous," she said, keeping her voice low, not sure if it would carry down to the deer and scare them away.

He gave her a nod of approval. They stood beside each other until the deer disappeared, until the sun began to sink behind the mountains. Tiny little lights blinked on and off down in the valley, close to the tree line.

She laughed with delight. "Fireflies. I haven't seen those since I was a little girl."

A half smile played around his mouth. "They've always been here. You just have to know where to look."

"You grew up here?" She waved her hand to encompass the incredible vista surrounding them. "With all of this?"

He nodded. "Tennessee, the real Tennessee, the one the tourists never stop long enough to appreciate, is heaven on earth. I can't imagine any place more beautiful. I left for a few years to go to college, see a bit of the world. But my heart was always here. No matter where I go, I'll always come back to Destiny."

"You haven't mentioned a family." As soon as

she said it, she worried that she might have stumbled into bad territory, that he might have memories in his past he'd like to forget, like she did. But the smile on his face told her otherwise. Family wasn't a bad memory for him. The love shining out of his eyes told her that, even without the smile.

"I reckon I'm related to half the people on this mountain," he teased. "I can't go anywhere without running into a second or third cousin, twice removed. And that's on top of my parents and three brothers. At church the Downings take up three pews. And we usually get together a couple of times a month at someone's house—potluck, everyone brings a dish. We roast marshmallows over an outdoor fire pit, tell ghost stories, swap lies about who caught the biggest fish last."

His smile faded as he looked at her. "I'm sorry. I shouldn't have gushed like that."

She shook her head. "Don't apologize. I asked. And I love hearing about your family, about your life out here. It sounds…wonderful. Tell me more."

The moon was high in the sky and the stars burning bright by the time they retreated inside, driven in by the no-see-ums, gnats and other flying bugs that descended onto the balcony, attracted by their presence.

Chris stopped beside her bed and gave her a soft kiss on her forehead. "You have to be starving by now. Are you a carnivore or one of those vegan people?" He shuddered, as if not eating meat was a fate worse than death.

"I can eat a steak with the best of them," she reassured him. "But I'm not hungry just yet. I think I'll just lie down a little bit longer, if that's okay."

"Of course. I'll be in the next room, just a knock on the wall away."

He started to turn away, but she tugged his hand, keeping him there. His brows raised in question.

She stood on her tiptoes and reached up and cupped his handsome face in her hands. The aching need she'd felt for him back in the chief's office, when they'd shared that soul-shattering kiss, was nothing compared to the way her heart yearned for him now.

There was something so adorable about this man, something that called out to her in every way. He was so kind, took such joy in the world around him. Her bruised and battered soul, even with everything still going on, seemed to feel better, to heal just a little bit more, every time she was around him. She couldn't just let him leave without knowing what he meant to her at this moment. Or how amazing it was to meet a man who put everyone else first, no matter what. That kind of selflessness was rare, a true gift, to be treasured, cherished.

She angled her lips up toward him, waiting, hoping. He was too tall for her to reach unless he wanted this, too. His eyelids dropped to half-mast, need and hunger reflected in his eyes as he leaned down and pressed his lips against hers.

But this was her kiss. She wanted to lead, and he let her. She kissed him, softly, gently, as he'd kissed her back at the station. She poured all the sweetness into her kiss, the raw, new emotions she felt for him but couldn't yet define. She tried to show him that she cared, that he mattered to her, so much that it confused her. All she knew was that he'd saved her life, but he was also saving her soul.

When he would have deepened the kiss, it nearly killed her to pull away. But she wasn't ready for more, not yet. She needed to think and rest and try to make sense of things.

The question was there in his eyes. She fanned her fingers over his cheeks, smiling up at him.

"I wasn't ready for you," she whispered. "You're a surprise. My heart..." She shook her head and smoothed her fingers across his shirt. "Thank you."

The poor man looked just as confused as she felt.

"Thank you for saving me, several times," she said. "Thank you for being there for me no matter what, for sharing the joy of your childhood, your family, your love for this mountain. But most of all, thank you for sharing your pain. I'm so sorry that you lost someone you loved. But it means more than you can possibly know that you shared that with me. It gives me hope that I can work through my own losses, move on and be...happy...one day. So, thank you."

She kissed him again, then dropped her hands and got into bed. She pulled the covers up to her chin. "I really am tired. I think everything that's happened has exhausted me. I'll just lie here awhile longer, okay?"

He looked like he wanted to say something, then sighed and changed his mind about whatever it was.

"I'll be in the next room if you need anything." He waved toward a closed door beside the nightstand. "That's the bathroom. The bag that Donna packed for you is in there."

After he left and pulled the door closed, she shut her eyes. All of his talk about family and happy times had lifted her up, but it also had her thinking about her own family, and feeling like a traitor for laughing and smiling after what had happened to them.

She tried to remember her family the way they'd been before her mother's alleged overdose, before her father supposedly shot himself, before Naomi's mysterious illness. And, mostly, she just tried to remember her family before Alan Webb injected himself into their lives and destroyed them all.

CHRIS HAD BEEN standing over the cabin's kitchen table for about an hour now, moving papers back and forth, like pieces of a puzzle, but so far, he wasn't able to see the big picture.

The background information was pouring in, thanks to the emails and phone calls from his team. But, no matter how he looked at everything or how he classified it into various lists, he wasn't seeing the connections that he needed to make.

He straightened and rubbed the back of his neck. It looked like the only thing to come out of tonight's research session was an aching back and a crick in his neck.

The sound of feet padding across the carpet had him turning around to see Julie coming toward him. She'd changed into a tank top and shorts, revealing a mouthwatering amount of smooth, pale skin. Normally he was all about eyes, lips and curves. But Julie's legs were incredible and had him picturing how they'd feel wrapped around his waist while he—

"Turn around," she said. "And sit. I can help you with that stiff neck you were rubbing."

Since he didn't think he could speak right now without his tongue lolling out, he decided to do what she said. He sat. The moment he did, she slid her hands onto his shoulders and began rubbing and kneading them in slow circles, working out the tension that had coiled in his muscles without him even realizing it.

When she moved her hands to his neck and began massaging him again, his head dropped toward his chest and he let out a groan of pure ecstasy.

She laughed and continued her ministrations.

"You're really good at this." He closed his eyes, hoping she'd never stop.

"I'm good at a lot of things."

Her sexy whisper near his ear had his eyes flying

open. Did she realize how her words sounded? The double meaning his suddenly lust-fogged mind had latched on to? He waited, barely breathing. When she didn't say anything else or lead him toward the bedroom, he silently berated himself for even thinking of her that way. He desperately wanted to make love to her, but that would be completely inappropriate.

The few kisses they'd shared were just as inappropriate, but he blamed them on the fact that they were both tired and not thinking straight. He couldn't use that excuse now. It was nearly ten o'clock at night, which meant she'd taken a three hour nap. And he'd slept for at least two hours on the couch before coming into the kitchen to work on the case.

Julie was a witness, and she needed time to work through the topsy-turvy changes in her life. Chris had no business thinking of her except as a woman he was duty-bound to protect.

Too bad his traitorous body wasn't listening.

His phone buzzed on the table. With Julie's hands still massaging his neck, he carefully leaned forward and picked up the phone. And just like that, the lust-induced fog evaporated. He reached up and took one of her hands in his, pulling her away from him.

"Thanks. Really," he told her. "But I've got to answer this."

The disappointment in her eyes had him wondering if maybe he *hadn't* imagined the sexy double entendre of her earlier words. And that made taking this call feel like torture.

He cleared his throat, gave Julie a pained smile as he held the phone against his ear. "Hi, Mom."

Julie's eyes widened. Then she started to laugh.

He frowned at her, which only made her laugh harder.

"No, Mom. No, I'm, ah, working." He listened to her next question and shook his head. "No, that's not Donna that you just heard. You don't know this woman." He shook his head again as his mother continued to badger him with questions. "No, it's not Nancy the 911 operator either. Nancy works from home, Mom. Yes, you can route 911 calls remotely these days." He rolled his eyes.

Julie grinned and blew him a kiss before retreating into the bedroom.

Chris groaned.

His mother demanded to know if he was hurt or something.

"What? Oh, no, sorry, Ma. I'm fine, promise. Are you okay? It's awful late. What? You can't sleep? Okay. Me? Just working a case—you know, same old, same old. Church? Oh, sorry. I forgot." He closed his eyes. Shoot. He had completely forgotten to call her and tell her he wouldn't make it to church.

While he listened to his mother go on and on about how important it was to go to church, he settled back and rested his head against the wood slats of the chair. Missing church was a cardinal sin in his mother's book. She would probably be up all night praying for his eternal soul. And if she had her way, he'd be up, too, listening while she prayed.

He sighed and shoved back from the table. The cool night air this high up on the mountain had put a definite chill inside the family room. He knelt down by the fireplace, saying the occasional "Yes, ma'am" into the phone whenever his mother paused for breath. Once he had a roaring fire going, he settled onto the massive sectional couch and rested his head on one of the throw pillows.

This was going to be a long night.

Chapter Nineteen

The deep, husky sound of Chris's voice had faded long ago. He must have finally finished his phone call. But, unfortunately, he hadn't taken Julie's hint and joined her in the bedroom. Or maybe he had taken the hint, and the answer was no.

Sighing, she stared at the ceiling above her bed, the moonlight flooding in through the high-set windows giving her plenty of light to see by. The idea of making love to Chris Downing, once it had settled in her mind, wouldn't go away. She didn't need to know him for years to know he was a good man and that she was wildly attracted to him. In a matter of days she knew he was a far better person than she could ever hope to be, and had her thinking all kinds of what-ifs.

She looked toward the doorway. The kitchen light had been turned off long ago, replaced with the flickering of firelight. While her bedroom was warm with the heavy comforter surrounding her, the appeal of that fire beckoned, if only because Chris was out there, too.

Thumping the bed impatiently, she debated her options. Lie here all night, unable to sleep, wishing she was with Chris. Or go see whether he wanted her as much as his kisses implied. The worst he could do was say no. She'd be mortified, but she'd never heard of anyone really dying from embarrassment. And at least she wouldn't be lying here for the rest of the night wondering whether she'd blown her chance.

Decision made, she tossed back the covers before she chickened out and changed her mind. She opened the nightstand drawer, knowing what she would find. She'd looked in it earlier while hoping that Chris would follow her. After grabbing one of the foil packets, she padded across the carpet and into the family room.

The gorgeous fireplace was like a beacon, the flames dancing across real wood logs, heat flooding into the room. It was beautiful and made the gas-burning fireplace in her Nashville home seem like a pathetic pretender in comparison. But when she rounded the end of the brown leather sectional that faced the fireplace, she froze in awe.

There were so-called masterpieces hanging in her home, but none of them came close to framing the incredible male beauty before her. Chris must have gotten overheated from the fire. He'd shed his clothes, all except his boxers. With one arm crooked over his head, the muscles of his chest were displayed to advantage, golden light flickering across his skin.

A light matting of dark hair furred his chest and marched down the center of his abs to disappear beneath the waistband of his underwear. One of his legs was drawn up, his other hand draped over his knee. Thickly muscled thighs tapered to his calves. Even his feet were sexy. Everything about him was enticing and, yet, so perfect, so beautiful, she could have stood there forever just drinking him in.

No, no, what she was doing was wrong. Watching him without him knowing it was like being a voyeur, a Peeping Tom. She should either wake him up and risk his rejection, or go back to her room. Option number three, standing here all night marveling at him as he slept, while incredibly appealing, was not an option at all. She needed to do something. Soon. Now.

Good grief, the man was gorgeous.

She sighed and bit her lip in indecision.

An intake of breath had her gaze shooting to his face. His eyes were open and he was watching her. He made no move to cover up or sit up. Instead, he simply waited, his jaw tight, his pupils dilated. Like a hungry panther, languidly watching its mate. Any thought of being rejected died in the face of such raw need. He wanted her, needed her, as much as she wanted and needed him.

Slowly, she crossed the room, devouring him with her eyes, her fingers clenching at her sides.

The foil crinkled in her grip. His gaze went to her hand, and when he saw what she was holding, his nostrils flared.

When she stopped in front of the couch, he held out his hands to her, an invitation she was helpless to resist. And then she was beneath him, the delicious weight of his body pressing her down, his lips greedily moving across hers in an openmouthed kiss that had her moaning and panting even before his tongue swept inside.

A draft of cold air across her shoulders told her that he'd taken off her top. The man was an expert at undressing a woman. That both delighted and dismayed her. She didn't want to think about anyone who'd come before her—or the woman he'd professed to love back in his college days. She wanted this man completely to herself.

Before long they were both naked, heated skin sliding against heated skin. His hands were everywhere, caressing, molding, stroking, making her shiver with delight. She wanted to touch him as much as he wanted to touch her. They twisted and strained against each other, kissing and being kissed, touching and being touched.

Then he was pressing her down again, claiming her mouth with his. She vaguely registered the sound of the foil packet being torn. He must have taken it from her at some point. She didn't remember. He lifted off her, rolling the condom into place while he continued to make love to her mouth with his.

And then, just when she thought she would die if he didn't take her, he moved between her thighs, pressing against her.

She eagerly lifted her legs, cradling him against her body. When he didn't press into her, she opened her eyes to see why.

He was staring at her, his face inches from hers. He smiled, gently kissed her, then framed her face in his hands.

"You're so beautiful, and strong, and brave," he whispered. "Are you sure about this? We haven't known each other that long. I'm supposed to be protecting you, not...doing this."

She slid her fingers across his ribs, making him shudder against her. "I'm more sure about this than anything in my whole life. Don't stop, Chris. Love me. Please. Just love me."

He shuddered again and swooped down to kiss her, his tongue thrusting between her lips as he thrust inside her body. The pleasure, the pressure of him filling her so completely while he did amazing things with his mouth and his hands had her arching off the couch, whimpering against him.

He tore his mouth from hers, his eyes squeezed shut, his jaw tight as he pumped into her, over and over, drawing her body into a tight bow of pleasure. She kissed the column of his throat, scored her nails down the muscles of his back, encouraging him with the words of lovers passed down through the generations.

Higher and higher he drew her up on waves of pleasure so exquisite she didn't think she could possibly go any higher. And then, with one clever stroke of his fingers, a deep thrust of his body inside hers, he took her to a new level.

He let out a savage growl and captured her mouth with his before sliding both hands beneath her bottom and angling her up. He withdrew once more, then plunged into her so deeply she exploded, shouting his name as she clung to him, her body shuddering with the strength of her climax. He thrust into her again, riding her through the waves of pleasure until he tightened inside her and came apart in her arms, his breath rushing out of him in a groan of ecstasy and making her climax all over again.

Like embers from a wildfire, they both slowly floated back to earth, wrapped in each other's arms, skin slicked with sweat. She could feel his heart hammering in his chest, feel the rush of her own pulse slamming in her veins.

He shuddered again, then slowly withdrew, turning her in his arms, spooning her with a thigh draped over hers as he turned them toward the fireplace. Her eyes fluttered closed. Her body felt boneless, cradled against his. He curled an arm over her belly, his fingers idly caressing the undersides of her breasts. She fell asleep with him whispering erotic love words in her ear and telling her how beautiful she was.

Chapter Twenty

Chris fanned the papers out on the kitchen table, trying again to refocus on the case and look at all of the clues in light of the latest reports he'd gotten just after the sun came up.

He glanced toward the ground floor bedroom. Julie was still getting ready to face the day, putting on makeup that he'd assured her she didn't need. For some reason, that had only made her more determined to fix her makeup and do something with her hair. He shook his head and looked down at the papers.

After making love twice more during the night, they'd both been exhausted and famished. They'd cooked omelets at four in the morning, taking turns feeding each other, laughing like a couple of newlyweds, before hopping into the shower together. If he wasn't careful, he could easily fall in love with the amazing woman.

The thought of his first love, Sherry, shot through his mind. Losing her had been devastating. Losing

Julie? He couldn't even go there. It would destroy him. Maybe it was already too late to guard himself from caring too much. But it wasn't too late to protect her. He had to figure out who her late husband had been working with and why. If he didn't do that, he could never guarantee her safety.

He studied the newest list he was making, the same one that he'd started in the chief's office but never finished. This time he had more information.

Love.
Money.
Revenge.
Hatred.
Hide something.

Those were the possible motives he was working with.

Love. He hesitated. Did Julie love someone else? Was she involved with someone in Nashville? As soon as those thoughts went through his head, he discarded them. She was so honest with her feelings. There was no way that she could have made love with him last night, giving herself to him so completely, if she loved someone else. Her ex hadn't tried to kill her because of some love triangle. He crossed that one off the list.

Next possible motivation—*money.* Yesterday, he'd have been inclined to cross this one off the list, too. But that was before he'd received the in-depth financial study on Alan Webb and his family's import-export business. Everything was coming together now. And money seemed to be at the root of the whole damn thing.

"You look like you've got the weight of the whole world on your shoulders."

He looked up to see Julie crossing the kitchen toward him. Today she was wearing a blue blouse tucked into blue dress slacks, showing off all her curves. Her shoulder-length hair hung in glossy waves, with a simple side part. She didn't seem to be wearing much makeup, but what she did have on emphasized her eyes and her dark lashes, making him want to sit for hours just staring at her.

"Have I told you how beautiful you are?"

Her face flushed a delightful pink. "About a dozen times. Thanks." She cleared her throat. "What are you working on?"

He forced his gaze to the paper in front of him. "Finances. Specifically, you and your husband's. Did you know that his family's business was teetering on the brink of bankruptcy before you married him?"

She frowned. "That can't be right. Alan always had money in college. I think that's how he got a lot of people to like him—free drinks all around whenever he was in a bar. He never once said anything about running short on cash, or mentioned concerns about his father's company."

Chris shoved the financial report on Webb Enterprises across the table as she sat across from him.

"The company got a huge influx of cash from another corporation a few weeks after you got married."

Her brows furrowed as she skimmed the pages of the report. "What was the payment for?"

"It was listed as cash flow from an investment. But the state cops working on the financial side of the investigation can't find where any companies have invested in Webb Enterprises to produce revenue anywhere close to that amount. And the payments have continued, once a month, for years. Until recently, when they suddenly stopped."

She glanced up. "They stopped? When?"

"On your twenty-fifth birthday."

Her eyes widened. "My birthday? That's...a coincidence. Odd, but what other explanation could there be? What was this other corporation?"

"Victoria and Edward."

She blinked, her face going pale. "My grandmother's business?"

He nodded.

"Let me get this straight. My estranged grandmother, Elizabeth Victoria Abbott, the one who disowned my mother and never made any attempt to have anything to do with us, has been making cash payments to my husband ever since I got married? Is that what you're saying?"

"That's exactly what I'm saying."

"But...I never heard anything about it. Wait, wait." She held up a hand as if to stop him, a panicked look entering her eyes. "You said Webb Enterprises was going broke. But then my...grandmother...began making those payments. Then, all this time, Alan wasn't the wealthy one. It wasn't his business that was buying our fancy house and fancy cars. It was my distant relative in London?"

He nodded. "That's what it looks like."

She fisted her hands on the table. "Money. You said one of the motives for murder is money. And you said that you don't believe in coincidences."

"Right." He watched her work through what he'd been working through all morning. He didn't have all the answers, but this was the biggest piece so far. It had to be the key. He waited to give her time to process everything, and to be there for her once she did.

Several minutes went by. When she looked at him again, the tears that he'd expected to see weren't there. Instead, she looked almost...relieved.

"So that's the answer then," she said. "That's why our marriage was so rocky, right from the start. Alan didn't marry me for love. He married me for money. Which is incredibly ironic considering his parents always acted like they thought I'd married him for his money." She shook her head. "This is crazy. Alan had to have been insane, a psychopath. He somehow knew about the link between my family and this corporation of my grandmother's and...what? Tried to figure out how to get the money? Oh, God above. It all makes sense now."

She pressed a hand to her stomach.

"What you said yesterday," she continued, "everything on the board—it's all true, and it all makes a horrible, macabre sense. Alan needed money. He found out about my grandmother, somehow. Then he hit on my sister. But she didn't like him. He must have realized he couldn't manipulate her so, instead, he killed her, and then my parents, leaving me as the one link to my grandmother. Let me guess. She regrets disowning my mother and set up a trust or something, right? You said she's still alive, so it can't be a simple inheritance. But it must still be set up to pay the heir—which, with the rest of my family dead— is me. Did I get it right, Chris? Alan knew he could manipulate me, so he killed everyone else? That's it, isn't it?"

Her voice broke and she closed her eyes, drawing in deep breaths.

Chris hurried to her, crouching in front of her. He wanted to draw her into his arms, hold her. But her stiff posture and the expression on her face told him she wouldn't welcome his touch right now. She needed time to work it through. He would wait all day if he had to. And when she needed him, he would be here.

She sat there, her back ramrod straight, for several minutes, before finally opening her eyes. She blinked at him, her eyes dry, her look determined.

"I need to hear you say it," she said. "Tell me I'm right, or tell me I'm wrong. Just say it."

"I'm sorry, Julie. But I think you're absolutely

right. The finance guys are trying to contact your grandmother and representatives at Victoria and Edward Corporation to get more details. But it might take a while to get that information. On this side of the pond, they've confirmed the amounts of the payments, when they began, when they stopped, the financial troubles at Webb Enterprises, which is again having trouble, by the way. They haven't been able to make payroll this past month. The company is again in jeopardy of going bankrupt."

Her lips curled with disdain. "Because, for some reason, the payments Alan was getting stopped on my birthday. Now his company, his parents' company, doesn't have that cash cushion every month so they're failing again."

"Seems like it, yes. The question of course is why the payments were made in the first place. What triggered them to start if your grandmother had disowned your mother? Somehow she or her lawyers must have found out about you and Naomi and she decided to send you money. Maybe the payments were contingent on college graduation, or getting married." He shrugged. "If the payments were meant for you, why did someone set them up to go to Alan? And, more importantly, why did they stop on your birthday? If we can answers to those questions, we'll understand why Alan tried to kill you after you turned twenty-five."

"And why someone is still trying to kill me," she finished. "Alan's not the only partner in this endeavor. You've been saying all along that he had to be working with someone else. That would explain why those men tried to kill us at Cooper's farm. They have to finish what Alan started. And if it's been about the money all this time, I have to think their goal is to get the payments going again."

"I doubt that's their goal."

She crossed her arms, resting them on the table in front of her. "I thought we agreed this is all about money."

"Oh, absolutely. It's definitely about money, even if some other motivations are coming into play. But if you've been—pardon my analogy—a cash cow all this time, why kill you if it's about the monthly payments? They've stopped already, and yet your life is still in danger. That has to mean some kind of cash payout. Maybe the monthly payments were part of a trust, and you're to get the full lump sum at age twenty-five."

She nodded. "Okay, okay. That could make sense. If there's a trust and I'm the sole heir, when I turn twenty-five I have to…do something? To get the lump-sum payout? But since I don't know, or didn't know, about the trust, Alan had to do something else." Her eyes widened. "He would be *my* heir. If I died, he would get the lump sum. Isn't that how these things work?"

Again, Chris shook his head. "In general, yes. But I don't see that as the explanation here. If it were as simple as killing you and making Alan the heir, he—"

"Would have killed me right after we got married," she finished.

He nodded. "Yes. I think he would have."

She got up and began pacing back and forth. "Alan needed me alive to get the original payments. That implies proof of life to the trustees. How would he do that without me knowing about it?"

"I think we're back to the partner theory again. Someone, perhaps working with the trust, had to be working with Alan. Maybe he provided proof to that person and they claimed to have seen you in person. Here, take a look at this."

He shuffled through a stack of papers and pulled one of them out. "I printed this from an email this morning. Randy drove to Nashville last night and worked with the local PD there to search your house. He brought a locksmith, too, who opened the safe. And this paper shows the contents."

She read the paper. "Birth certificates, for my parents, my sister, me." She pressed a hand against her throat. "Death certificates for my family. My marriage license?"

"I imagine these are what he used to get the payments started. But he wouldn't need them after that. So I doubt this is what he wanted when he came to Destiny looking for you."

"No, probably not," she agreed. She swallowed hard. "I'm not an expert on trusts. But I'm thinking they can be written up any way the maker of the trust wants. If my grandmother was holding wealth for my

mother's heir, these birth and death certificates prove
that I'm the heir. And the marriage license proves
that Alan was my husband. Since my grandmother
never made any attempt to see me or my family in
person, she was probably perfectly willing to ac-
cept that I would feel the same way. Her trustees, or
perhaps the partner we keep theorizing about, were
fine accepting Alan as their surrogate. Pay Alan,
they were paying me. The requirements of the trust
are satisfied without any messy family reunions."

The bitterness in her voice had Chris pulling her
into his arms without thinking. Instead of stopping
him, she sank against him, holding on to him as he
rocked her and stroked her hair. They sat that way
for a long time, until she let out a shuddering breath
and pulled back.

She kissed him, a sweet, soft kiss that rocked him
to his soul.

"Thank you," she said. "I don't think I could get
through this without you. It's a heavy burden, a lot to
take in. If it weren't for you, I probably would have
curled up in a fetal position long ago and given up."

He shook his head and squeezed her shoulders.
"No. You wouldn't have done that. You're far too
strong. Alan used you, he destroyed your family.
Now he's dead. And I'm not going to apologize for
saying that I'm glad he's dead."

She smiled. "I think I'm kind of glad he's dead,
too, even though that sounds terrible." Her smile
faded. "Where do we go from here? I still don't un-

derstand why someone else is after me or how Alan got this started without someone verifying it with me."

"That's definitely a piece we need to figure out. Plus we need to find out what's required by the trust once you attained age twenty-five to get the lump sum payout, which is the only thing that makes sense to me. Alan wanted you alive to get payments, but once you reached twenty-five, something changed and the payments stopped. At that point, he was still trying to get something from you. So that implies you have something he needed in order to get the lump sum."

She nodded. "But now that he's dead, his partner needs me dead. Why?"

"To cover their tracks I'm guessing. Since they're trying to kill you, not talk to you like Alan tried, then they've either found another way to get the money or they've given up on that and just want to ensure you can't lead anyone to them. Did your husband have your power of attorney? That could help explain how he got the trust to give him the payments in the first place."

"I never gave him a power of attorney. He never even asked."

Chris nodded. "It probably would have raised red flags to you if he'd asked right after you got married. I'm guessing he already had that part covered. Maybe he had a forger produce one for him. As much diabolical planning as he did in regards to your family, a simple power of attorney couldn't have been more than a blip on his radar."

She sighed. "True."

"When our finance guys cut through the red tape and get a copy of the trust document, that should clear up a lot of our questions and hopefully will point us in the right direction to figure out who was Alan's partner."

"One of the main things bugging me," Julie said, "is Harry Abbott. It can't be a coincidence that he shares my last name. Have you found anything else about him?"

"He appears to be your distant cousin, on your mother's side obviously, hence his last name. The team is still working on how that might figure on the case. Brian Henson, the one driving the black Charger, has to be another hit man your husband hired. Which means this still all seems to tie into the ADA somehow since Henson was her assistant. The team will need to look into Bolton, too, the other admin assistant, just in case he's part of this. If Nelson was Alan's partner, she may be tying up loose ends to make sure none of this comes back to bite her, especially given her political aspirations. Maybe she's the one who hired the hit men instead of your husband. Maybe she's protecting herself."

He gently lifted her off his lap and set her on her feet. "I'm going to talk all this through with Max. He's managed to cull some amazing contacts by networking at seminars and conferences. Maybe one of those contacts can put some pressure on your grand-mother or the attorney's running the trust to get the information that we need. Maybe she can answer questions about Harry Abbott, too. Plus, we need to look into Kathy Nelson, see if we can tie her to any of this."

She nodded and moved to stand by one of the win-dows, looking out onto the mountains.

Chris called Max and brought him up to speed.

"Hold on," Max said through the phone. "The chief wants to tell me something."

Chris shoved back from the table and meandered around the furniture to Julie's side. He put his arm around her shoulders and pulled her against him as they looked at the achingly beautiful day, how the sun shone down onto the trees and mountains.

He was glad that he'd brought her here. He'd never intended to talk shop in the cabin, but they'd made a lot of progress. They could sit back now, enjoy the seclusion, enjoy each other and let her continue the healing process while his team caught up to Hen-son and looked into Nelson's dealings. A few days in the mountains without any other cabins for miles around could be exactly what Julie needed. Chris too. Because he was finding out that she was exactly what he needed.

As soon as Max came back on the phone and told him what the chief had said, Chris swore and grabbed Julie's hand.

"We're leaving—now," he told Julie and Max at

the same time. He pulled Julie toward the bedroom while he worked out the planned route with Max. "That's right, we'll head down now and meet you in—Max? Max? You still there?"

He pulled the phone away from his ear. The signal still showed strong, but the phone had only static. He swore again, shoved the phone into the holder on his belt and grabbed the duffel from beside the bed.

"What's going on?"

The fear in Julie's voice made him hesitate. "A state cop was killed a few minutes ago after pulling over a speeder at the bottom of this mountain. Another cop saw the patrol car on the side of the road and found the dead trooper. When he viewed the dash cam he saw that the cop had pulled over a black Camaro. As he was walking up to the driver's window, a black Charger raced past and the driver shot the officer. The Camaro pulled out behind the Charger and they both took off down the road. It was Henson and Bolton. And the road they were on is the only one up this mountain."

"Oh, my God."

"Put your shoes on. We're leaving." After double-checking the guns and ammo in the duffel bag, he zipped it up and slung it over his shoulders like a backpack. He tightened the straps so it was snug and secure.

Julie had just put on her second shoe when the throaty roar of a powerful engine sounded from outside, then abruptly shut off.

Chris raced to the window.

The Charger was in the driveway. The Camaro was parked a little farther down the road.

Both cars were empty.

Chapter Twenty-One

Julie was shaking so hard she could barely keep her balance on the balcony stairs. Chris was right behind her, pistol in his right hand, left hand gripping the waistband on the back of her pants like a lifeline in case she lost her footing.

The front door to the cabin had burst open right after Chris had looked out the bedroom window. He'd fired several shots through the bedroom doorway and thought he might have nicked Henson on the shoulder. Chris had slammed the door shut and shoved the nightstand against it. Then he was urging Julie through the back hallway to the balcony.

It was bad enough knowing two hit men were looking for them and could suddenly appear from out of nowhere. Worse was trying not to panic at what waited for them down below. Julie tried to keep her eyes on the stairs, not the stilts under the house to her left that kept it from plunging down the side of the mountain. And certainly not on the fact that the stairs appeared to end several feet above the ground—

ground that was steep and littered with razor-sharp-looking rocks. One wrong move and both of them would be killed.

"Stop," Chris ordered, jerking her back toward him.

She froze, her foot suspended in the air above the last step. He eased down to the stair beside her, then slammed his shoe against the step she'd been about to use. It exploded in a rain of sawdust and splintered wood.

"Dry rot," he whispered.

She shivered, wondering what would have happened if she'd been standing on that step when it collapsed. Since the pieces of wood from it were still bouncing down the side of the mountain, she really didn't have to wonder all that much. She swallowed, hard.

"Why do they even have these stairs if they don't reach all the way to the ground anyway?" She knew she sounded like a petulant child, but she was so tired of running and being shot at and having the constant threat of death hanging over her head. Surely she was allowed to complain every once in a while.

"There were probably another half-dozen stairs at one time. It's to provide access for examining the structure beneath the house and the foundation, to make sure it's secure."

He looked up behind them. Julie didn't see any signs of a gunman, but Chris's jaw tightened and he looked around, back toward the stilts, as if time was running out. One last glance down the mountain, then back to the stilts.

"Hold on to the railing," he whispered. "Don't move." He lifted his leg and grabbed a gun from his ankle holster, then shoved it into her front left pants pocket. "Just in case."

She made a choking sound in her throat. "In case of what?"

He looked back at the stilts again.

"Wait," she called out. "That's a six-foot leap, at least. And if you miss the tiny strip of land below us, you'll plunge off the side of the mountain. Please tell me you aren't going to try to—"

He jumped from the stairs, pushing off so hard the entire staircase wobbled.

Julie sucked in a breath and clung to the railing, staring in horror as Chris clung to the bottom stilt, trying to pull himself up on a crossbar. Dots swam in her vision and she realized she was still holding her breath. She forced herself to draw in some air while she sent up an anxious prayer for his safety.

He managed to get his fingertips around the crossbar, then pulled himself up to standing. He was about a foot above her now, but still a good six feet away. It might as well have been the Grand Canyon.

"Keep an eye out," he warned as he began unfastening his belt.

She looked at the balcony above them. "I don't see anyone."

"Good. Slide over to this side of the stairs. Hurry."

He yanked out his belt and threaded the end through the buckle, then looped the other end of the belt around his wrist and back on itself, grasping the end in his palm.

She did as he'd asked and looked down. "The ground isn't too far away. Maybe I can jump."

"No. It's too rocky, too steep. Your momentum will throw you right off the cliff."

"Cliff?" She leaned over, then jerked back. "Oh. Yeah. The cliff. This is why I love Nashville and don't live in the country. I remember now."

He grinned. "You might have a point. It's not really a cliff. More like a really steep hill with lots of rocks. Still, taking a ride down there wouldn't be my first choice."

"Or mine."

After another quick glance up, he looked over his shoulder toward the house where the stilts were cut into the side of the mountain, essentially bolting the house in place. What was Chris's plan, for them to both cling to the stilts until help arrived? That might be great for him, but she'd never make it. Her legs were too short.

"You can make it," he said, as if hearing her thoughts. "I'm going to swing my belt toward you. Catch it and slide your hand in the loop. Then tighten it back until it hurts. I'm serious. Make it as tight as you can. I don't want your hand falling through."

"Maybe I could just go up the stairs and take my

chances inside. They might not expect me to have a gun."

"They're hit men, Julie. They kill people for a living. They're probably better shots than I am. You really want to take that chance?"

She clutched the railing and looked down again. "Not really. But I don't want to become a human pancake, either."

He laughed. "You're adorable, you know that?"

"I'll bet you say that to all the women you drop down the sides of mountains."

"Counting you? You're right." He shrugged, then winked. "Come on. The only reason Henson hasn't come out that door with guns blazing already is he's giving me more credit than I deserve. He probably thinks I'm waiting on the balcony with a plan to ambush him."

"That might work."

"If it was just me, that's what I'd do. But there's no cover. You'd end up shot in the cross fire. Come on, Julie. Grab the belt."

Before she could think of another argument, he dropped down, hanging from the crossbar by his knees and swung the belt toward her. She grabbed it on the first try and quickly shoved her arm through the loop like he'd told her.

The belt was taut between them, pulling them toward each other, her left wrist looped in one end, his left looped in the other.

"Is your hand tight?" he called out. "So tight it feels like it's cutting off the circulation?"

"As a matter of fact, yes. I probably should loosen—"

The belt jerked and she was falling through the air. She would have screamed, but she slammed against Chris so hard the breath was knocked out of her. He grabbed her with both arms and shoved her up toward the beam, grunting at the effort as he hung upside down.

She gasped and scrambled onto the wood, grabbing another piece perpendicular to the one she was on and clinging to it for dear life. The belt slackened on her wrist. Chris had pulled his hand out of the other end. Then he swung himself up beside her and grinned like a little boy at Christmas after getting a new bat and ball.

"That was cool, wasn't it?"

"Cool?" she muttered. "We could have died. That was the scariest thing I've ever done in my life."

His eyes widened as he looked past her.

She whirled around to see a man bent over the top of the balcony, holding the biggest, scariest-looking gun she'd ever seen. And he was pointing it at her and Chris.

"Hang on," she heard Chris yell as automatic gunfire exploded all around them.

She grabbed for the crossbar.

And missed.

Suddenly she was free-falling into open air.

CHRIS LEAPED AFTER JULIE, twisting in midair, firing his pistol toward the gunman on the balcony. The rocky side of the mountain rushed up to meet them. He twisted again, jerking the end of the belt as hard as he could. She screamed and fell against his chest. He grabbed her just as his back slammed against the rocky side of the mountain.

Red-hot fire scraped across his back in the places unprotected by the duffel bag as they half skidded, half fell down the steep face. He used every ounce of his strength to try to keep Julie on top of him to protect her from the rocks, while scrabbling with his boots to try to slow them down.

"Chris!"

Julie's choked-out scream of warning had him twisting again to see a tree rushing up to meet them. He jerked sideways, rolling to avoid the deadly obstacle. A garbled yell told him she'd been scraped hard. Again and again, he twisted, jerked, shuffled his arms and feet, fighting against physics and the forces of nature to try to protect his precious burden.

Finally the rolling and twisting slowed. Their shoes slammed against the earth, pulling them both up short. They flopped end over end, like rag dolls, into the tree line. The sudden cessation of sound and movement did nothing to stop the world from spinning. Chris squeezed his eyes shut, willing the dizziness to go away.

A pained moan had him opening his eyes. He was flat on his back and what was left of the duffel. Julie was clutched in his arms, her hair a tangled mess of leaves and twigs. She moaned again, and he forced himself to roll over, hissing in a breath at the throbbing fire his back and side had become.

He laid her down on the grass and smoothed her hair. A tiny line of blood trickled from the corner of her mouth. Her eyes were closed.

"Julie, can you hear me, sweetheart? Julie?"

Crack!

The ground kicked up beside him in a puff of green and brown.

He jerked back, looking up toward the house, high upon the mountainside above them. A lone gunman stood on the balcony, leaning over the railing, calmly aiming a rifle.

Chris swore and scooped Julie into his arms. He dove behind a tree as more rifle fire cracked around them. On hands and knees, he shuffled deeper into cover until he was certain they were protected. Then he carefully laid her down once again.

...ied to wake her up, but she didn't respond other than to moan in pain if he moved her.

Please, God. Don't let her die. Please.

He pressed his hand against her chest, judging her breathing. It was steady, strong. A check of her pulse reassured him it, too, was strong. Then why wasn't she awake? He ran his fingers through her horribly tangled hair, feeling for bumps. When he touched behind her right ear, she gasped and arched away from him.

He almost cried in relief.

That little arch of her back told him at least she wasn't paralyzed.

Thank you, God.

His hand came away bloody. He leaned down, clamping his jaw shut to keep from crying out himself. His back was on fire, mostly on his left side. But he'd worry about that later.

Bending over her, he pulled her hair away from her neck. The cut on her scalp wasn't deep, but it was ragged and bleeding heavily, as head wounds usually did. He worked the duffel bag off his back and dropped it beside them on the ground. When he saw the first-aid kit in the bottom, he couldn't help smiling. He owed Max big-time for packing the duffel, and doing it right.

A few minutes later, he had Julie's head wound packed and bandaged. The bleeding already appeared to be slowing down from the pressure of the wrap. He continued searching for other injuries. Her side had been badly scraped, probably from when he'd had to roll to avoid the tree. Nothing much he could do about that except to spray it with antibiotics for now. Like a burn, if he tried to cover it up, it would just lead to infection.

A sharp intake of breath had his gaze shooting to Julie's face. Her eyes were open.

He let out a shaky laugh as he leaned over her.

"What's your name?" he asked.

"Chris."

"That's my name. What's your name?" he asked again.

She shook her head, then pointed. "Chris, my God. Your side."

He frowned and looked down.

A piece of tree branch the diameter of a quarter had impaled him, from back to front, and was sticking out of his left side.

"Guess that explains why my back's on fire." He tried to laugh, but of course as soon as he saw the wound, it started throbbing and burning far worse than it had before.

"Tell me your name," he insisted yet again. He held up three fingers. "How many fingers do you see?"

"Julie and three. I'm fine. You're the one who's hurt." She started to get up, then groaned and lay back down. "The whole world is spinning."

"Concussion. We need to get you to a doctor."

She kept her eyes closed and sat up, then slowly opened them again. "It's better. What in the world happened? We fell over the cliff?"

"More like you fell and I dove." He'd probably aged thirty years watching Julie fall off that crossbar and fly down the mountain. If he'd jumped even a half second later he doubted he'd have reached her in time to cushion her fall when she hit the highest swell of ground. If the mountain had been any steeper, neither of them would have survived.

"Can you stand?" he asked.

"I think so."

Together they pushed and pulled until they were both on their feet.

Julie started laughing. "If I look half as bad as you do we won't have to worry about the wildlife out here. They'll run away as soon as they see us."

He grabbed the duffel, and half the contents fell out. The material had been shredded. Since he'd lost his pistol in the fall, he was relieved to see one in what remained of the bag. Unfortunately, the extra magazines were scattered somewhere on the mountain.

He holstered his gun and checked Julie's pocket where he'd put his backup gun. Amazingly, the gun was still there. It would have been perfect if there was a knife in the duffel, but the two knives he'd seen in it earlier had escaped somewhere during their wild ride.

Looking at the sun, he tried to get his bearings. "We'll head that way." He pointed to his left. "That's east. It should lead to the nearest road. But we'll have to be as quiet as possible and keep a lookout the whole way."

"Why? It's not like the gunmen are going to leap off the balcony and try to free-fall down the mountain like we did. There's no way they'll catch up to us."

"There was only one gunman on the balcony—Henson. Bolton is still out there somewhere. And if I were him, I'd be heading down the mountain road right now to cut us off."

"Then shouldn't we go west or north or something, anywhere but east?"

"If you didn't have a concussion, I didn't have a tree in my back, and we had supplies to last a week or two, absolutely. East is our only option. It's just a few miles. Let's go."

Chapter Twenty-Two

She was worried about him.

The injury in Chris's side looked excruciating. How was he even walking, let alone stepping over the downed trees in their path and keeping his balance on the uneven ground?

After a terse argument about not having time to tend to his wound, Chris had finally given in and let her do what she could in sixty seconds, no more. She'd sprayed it with the antibiotic he'd used on her earlier, then stuffed some gauze around the piece of branch where it protruded both in back and front.

He'd stood stiffly, barely moving through her ministrations, and then he'd gone about three shades paler. His eyes had been glazed with pain by the time she'd stopped. Even with the packing, he was bleeding steadily.

"We should stop. You're losing too much blood."

He shook his head and plodded on, occasionally looking up when the sky could be seen through the thick canopy overhead. The man was incredibly stubborn and amazing and wonderful. And it was tearing her heart into pieces watching him, knowing he would die before he'd give up, all because he wanted her to be safe.

Tears clouded her vision, but she briskly wiped them away. He'd told her she was strong and brave. She was neither of those things, but for him, she was damn well going to pretend. He didn't need one more thing to worry about, like trying to console her. Somehow she had to hold everything inside and protect him.

The weight of his backup gun, now strapped on her ankle courtesy of Chris's ankle holster, wasn't very reassuring. How was she supposed to protect Chris in a gunfight, against a man who killed for a living? Somehow, she'd have to figure it out though. Because Chris was getting weaker and weaker. No way was he going to be able to protect himself if the gunman caught up to them.

He wobbled, falling against a tree. She reached for him, but he shook her off, straightened and started forward again. How long could he keep this up? How long could he survive? And where the heck was their backup?

Chris's phone hadn't survived the fall down the mountain. But he'd spoken to Max right before Henson and Bolton had arrived. She and Chris were heading toward the same road that Chris had told Max they'd go to, albeit on foot instead of by car. Still, if the SWAT team cared about their friend and fellow officer, they should bring the cavalry up the mountain to find him. So where were they?

A small cracking noise sounded from somewhere up ahead.

Chris froze, reaching out his right hand to stop her. But she'd already stopped. They both stood as still as possible, breathing through their mouths to make as little noise as they could, waiting, watching, listening.

There. Another crack, slightly to the right, like someone's shoe crunching a dead, dry leaf or a twig.

He looked down, then to their left, motioning for her to follow. She walked where he walked, careful not to stray from the path. The woods, this mountain, was his domain. But she was learning fast, emulating him, doing whatever it took to survive.

They stopped behind two thick trees, peering through the crack between them toward the sounds they'd heard. Chris slowly raised his pistol, leveling it in the opening, sighting his target.

A deer stepped out from the bushes.

Julie laughed and relaxed against the tree.

Chris frowned but kept his pistol trained, not moving.

Julie turned back toward the deer.

A dark shadow moved behind the bushes.

Bam! Bam! Bam! Chris fired six or seven times before he stopped.

Julie held her hand over her mouth, frozen in

place. A man staggered out onto the path, both hands red with blood as he held his stomach.

It was Henson.

"Help me." His plea was barely above a whisper. Then he dropped like a rock to the ground.

Chris grabbed Julie when she would have run to the other man.

"Don't. There's nothing you can do for him. And there's still one more gunman out there. Henson was on the balcony. He's the one who fired at us. If he found us, then the other guy has to be out here somewhere, too. And he's stalking us right now." He looked up at the sky. "Five, ten more minutes and we'll be at the road. If my team isn't already looking for us, we'll flag someone down. We're going to make it, Julie. Trust me."

He looked so haggard, so drawn, his complexion ashen. She wanted to weep. Instead, she smiled.

"I do. You'll take care of me. You always do." She looped her arm through his as if in comradery, when, really, she was just trying to hold him up.

His pistol was in his hand. She hop-skipped a few steps so she could grab hers from her ankle holster without stopping. Together, they headed deeper into the woods, side by side.

Rat-a-tat-tat-tat-tat!

Chris shoved her to the ground and dove on top of her. Bark and leaves exploded around them. Deafening automatic gunfire chewed into the trees near where they'd been standing.

Julie tried to bring her gun up, but his weight was pressing her wrist hard against the ground and she could barely move.

He fired toward the trees where the gunfire was coming from until his gun clicked. Out of bullets. He threw the gun to the ground. Then he was on his knees, lifting her, half-dragging her behind a tree.

Bullets sprayed the forest floor and the bark on the tree where he'd pulled her.

Then, suddenly, they stopped. Everything went quiet.

Chris was on his knees in front of her, his chest heaving with each breath he took. Blood coursed down his side, coating his arms, his hands. Julie was backed against the tree, holding the little ankle gun in her hands.

Crunching noises sounded to their left, their right. Was there more than one shooter now? And then the noise sounded directly behind Chris.

He stiffened.

Julie's breath froze in her lungs as Bolton stepped out from between the trees. The gun he held looked heavy, lethal, horrifying. It was a machine gun or something like that. All she knew for sure was that it was aimed at Chris's back.

"What do I do?" she whispered.

He gave her a half smile. "Live," he whispered. "Just live." He grabbed her gun and twisted around, using his body to shield her as he fired at Bolton.

Bam! Bam!
Boom!

The gunman blinked in shock, blood pouring from a hole at the base of his throat. Then he slowly crumpled to the ground.

Suddenly the woods filled with people: Randy, dressed in his SWAT gear, bending down to check the Bolton's pulse, shaking his head. Donna, also in SWAT gear, directing several state police, pointing back toward the path where the other gunman had gone down. Colby, staring in shock at Chris's side. And, finally, Max, dropping onto his knees beside Chris, who wasn't moving as Julie clutched him against her.

"Mrs. Webb, Julie, you have to let him go now." Max's voice was kind, gentle, like Chris's. "Let him go, so we can help him."

She looked at the precious man in her arms. His eyes were closed. Blood covered his back and made her arms sticky where she held him.

"Medic," Max yelled, as if they were in the middle of a combat zone.

Maybe they were.

Two EMTs rushed through the trees with a gurney.

"Julie. Let them help him," Max said. "You have to let him go."

His words seemed to reach her through a fog of pain and grief.

"Julie? Julie, are you okay?"

Max's voice had changed. He swore and again yelled, "Medic."

Julie surrendered to the darkness around her.

Chapter Twenty-Three

Julie couldn't believe that a month had passed since the shooting. And she also couldn't believe that she was once again sitting in the interview room at the Destiny Police Department, alone, waiting for others to join her.

She rubbed her left shoulder, trying to ease the ache where Bolton's bullet had passed through Chris's torso and buried itself in her upper arm. Both Chris and Max had shot Bolton. And since both of their bullets caused fatal injuries, they argued all the time over who should get the credit.

She smiled, glad to be alive, glad that Chris was alive. They were both still stiff and sore but would heal completely with time. She'd been released from the hospital a few days after admittance. But she'd still stayed, sleeping on a cot in Chris's room. Not that the two of them had any privacy.

Chief Thornton had assigned Detective Colby Vale to shadow her every move. He was essentially her bodyguard until they figured out who was trying to kill her. Thankfully, Colby was outside in the squad room right now, instead of in the interrogation room with her.

Chris had been released from the hospital yesterday. The skin on his back had been flayed away during their terrifying tumble down the mountain. He'd undergone several skin grafts. But at least he was up and walking, and finally allowed to leave the hospital.

She loved him. She'd realized that weeks ago during one of their many whispered talks in his hospital room, talks about everything from where they'd gone to kindergarten to their hopes and dreams. They hadn't talked about love yet, and she wasn't sure what the future held for them or if he felt about her the way she felt about him. The last month had focused more on recovery, and on wrapping up the case.

Which was why she was here. Chris had asked her to meet him at the station to discuss some new findings. She just wanted the case to be over and hoped this discussion meant that it finally was.

The door opened, and Chris stepped in, smiling as he crossed to the chair beside her.

"Hey, you," he said.

"Hey, yourself."

"Thanks for coming in," he said. "The chief will be here in just a minute."

"I can't believe you're already back at work. You aren't fully recovered yet. You should be home resting."

He shifted in his chair, the tension lines in his

face telling her she was right, that he was in pain, and had no business being here.

"I'm going to tell the chief to send you home. This is ridiculous. You need more time to heal." She started to push her chair back, but he stopped her with a hand on her arm.

"Julie, I'm not back at work, not full-time. I've only been working over the phone with the chief and the others trying to tie up the loose ends on your case. And we just got some crucial information that I believe is going to help us wrap this up once and for all."

She slowly settled back against her chair. "You know who's behind everything? Who sent the hitmen after me?"

"Not exactly."

She was about to ask him to explain what he meant when the chief stepped into the room and closed the door behind him.

He nodded in greeting. "Mrs. Webb. Thanks for coming in." He sat at the end of the small table.

"Okay," she said. "The suspense is killing me. And, although I really appreciate that you've got Colby playing bodyguard, I'd love to be able to walk down the street without having a policeman shadowing my every move. Is it Kathy? You've found evidence to prove she's behind everything?"

Chris took one of her hands in his. "We don't have definitive proof yet. But I've got an idea of how to get it. And it's based on information the team has pulled together over the past few weeks, plus some surveillance photos they've taken of Kathy Nelson. It all starts with your cousin, Harry Abbott."

Julie frowned. "I don't understand. It starts with him?"

"He's the key to this whole thing and how your husband was able to begin receiving payments from the trust without you ever knowing about it. Harry Abbott was a small-time lawyer. He worked for the law firm that your grandmother hired to handle the trust. Apparently your grandmother was very ill shortly before Naomi got sick. I don't know if that made your grandmother more aware of her mortality, or what. But that's when she sent Harry Abbott to try to locate her daughter and find out if there were any grandchildren. By the time she got information back, your family was gone. So she created the trust for you. It was supposed to start payments upon either college graduation or marriage."

"Seriously?" Julie said. "So if I didn't get enough education, or decided my life was perfectly fine without a man in it, she wouldn't have deemed me worthy of receiving any money?"

He shrugged. "She's old-fashioned. What can I say?"

"She sure is. Go on."

"Your grandmother said she hired that particular law firm to handle the trust because of your cousin. He was family and she preferred to keep things like that in the family."

"You've actually spoken to her?"

He nodded. "On the phone, yes. Once we got through the layers of assistants and bureaucracy to get to her, she was quite forthcoming. Like I said, Harry was assigned the task of tracking down your grandmother's American relatives on behalf of the trust. But the temptation of all that money was too much. He resented that his side of the family wasn't in the direct line to inherit, and he planned on getting his hands on that money, probably felt he deserved it. Once he located your family, he looked around for someone as diabolical as he was, and found Alan. They made a pact—that if Alan could marry into the family and help Harry provide proof to the trust regarding the heir, then they could share the monthly proceeds."

"How do you know all of this? Harry's dead."

The chief tapped the table to get her attention. "Extensive research and interviews with people who'd interacted with Harry when he was in the States. I don't like unsolved puzzles, and I'm not about to let some ADA abuse the trust of her constituents and give police a bad name without paying her debt to society. I threw half my police force at this. And we got results."

"Thank you," she said. "I sincerely appreciate it. But I'm even more confused than ever. I thought we were talking about my cousin. Now we're back to Kathy?"

Chris looked to the chief, who nodded, as if giving him permission to take up the story again.

"I'll try to get to the point," Chris said. "Harry colluded with Alan. But Alan wasn't having much luck with your family. Naomi didn't like him, so he decided you were his best chance. After eliminating your family, he apparently tried flirting with you but you were too distraught to notice. You did, however, have a friend you associated with—Kathy."

"So they did know each other before I met Alan," Julie said.

"Yes. The meeting at the football game was a setup. Alan and Harry were getting desperate so they brought her in as a way for Alan to get your attention. We believe, and it's backed up by financial records of Harry's accounts, that the monthly payments were split into thirds."

"Harry's accounts? Not Kathy's?"

"She's too clever for that. We think she's hiding her money offshore. She's slick. Hard to pin anything on her. But she's the only person who makes sense as a surviving partner who has something to lose if her role is exposed, thus the hitmen. Plus, now that we know the full requirements of the trust—including a clause about your twenty-fifth birthday that your grandmother amended four months before your birthday—we have a theory about what Kathy is trying to do to get that final lump sum."

"Four months before my birthday? Wait, that's

when things in my marriage took a nosedive, got really bad."

He nodded. "I know. I think that's when Harry broke the news to Alan."

She looked back and forth, from the chief to Chris. "What news?"

"That the payments would stop on your birthday unless you personally traveled to England to visit your grandmother, and that you bring the Abbott necklace with you—the one your mother gave to Naomi that used to belong to your grandmother. I'm pretty sure that's what Alan was looking for when he attacked you. He wanted the key to the safe so he could destroy the documents he had at your house. But he also wanted you to tell him where you had Naomi's things so he could get that necklace."

She held her hands up. "Wait. So not only did I have to finish college or get married in order to inherit, I also had to hold on to a necklace? What if I'd sold it, or lost it? I'd be out of luck?"

"Looks that way. Your grandmother is…a bit strict, uptight I guess. She really seems to value family and loyalty. I guess that's why it hurt her so much when your mother ran off with your father. It felt like a betrayal to her. And putting that stipulation about the necklace in the trust was her way of rewarding her heir only if they valued the history and legacy that necklace represented."

"You almost sound like you admire her," Julie accused.

"She's from a different generation, a different country, with a unique upbringing I could never understand. Let's just say that I'm trying to keep an open mind and see it from her perspective. Regardless, you can imagine Alan's reaction when he found out those details from Harry."

"He was probably furious. He couldn't take me to England, not without revealing what he'd been doing all this time. And, the necklace? No wonder he kept badgering me about my family's things. He needed to get the necklace without making me suspicious by specifically asking for it. Wait. It wouldn't do him any good without me though." She shook her head. "Did he think he could force me to lie to my grandmother? To not admit that Alan had been receiving the payments all along?"

Chris shot another look at the chief, then took both her hands in his this time. The concern on his face put her on edge.

"You're scaring me, Chris."

"I don't mean to. But the questions you're asking are exactly what I asked. And I don't believe for one minute that you would have meekly gone along with Alan's plan if that's what he wanted you to do. That's why Alan and his co-conspirators came up with a new plan. Alan was supposed to get the necklace from you. I think he was trying to get you to tell him where you kept your family's things without making you suspicious enough to kick him out or anything. Then, when you never revealed that information and you turned twenty-five—"

"He got desperate. Planned to kidnap me to force me to tell him."

"Right," Chris said. "But you foiled the first attack. I foiled the second. He never got a chance to get the necklace."

"Where does that leave us?" she asked.

The chief pulled a photograph from his suit jacket pocket. Chris let Julie's hands go and took the picture, placing it face down on the table in front of her.

"Hypothetically, if Alan could have gotten the necklace, then there was only one more thing he'd need after that—to take you to England with him. But he knew that wasn't an option, that you wouldn't go. So he and his co-conspirators had to make plans months ago in anticipation of your twenty-fifth birthday, for another way to fool your grandmother. Remember I said that the chief had someone performing surveillance on Kathy?"

She nodded, a sick feeling settling in her stomach. "Yes."

"She rented a house out in the country about three and a half months shy of your twenty-fifth birthday, two weeks after your grandmother changed the conditions of the trust. Apparently Kathy rented it for another woman, someone whom neighbors said was recovering from some kind of trauma, based on the bandages and the fact that nurses used to stop by every few days. She's fully recovered now. And this is what she looks like."

He flipped the picture over.

Julie pressed her hands against her mouth.

The woman in the picture looked exactly like Julie.

A WEEK LATER, Julie opened the front door of her Nashville home to admit her visitor. "Thank you for meeting me here. So many things have happened in the past few months and I've only been back in Nashville for a couple of days. It's good to see a familiar face." Julie stepped back, pulling the front door open for Kathy Nelson.

"Of course, of course." Kathy stepped inside. "I'm just so relieved that everything is settled. No more looking over your shoulder and wondering if someone is out to hurt you. I still can't believe Alan was after your money all along, and willing to kill you for it. I'm so very sorry that the men Alan recommended to me as assistants ended up being such horrible people, hitmen of all things. Of course I had no idea."

Julie forced a smile. "Yes. How could you have known? The whole thing is so hard to believe. I didn't even realize you and Alan had kept in touch over the years."

Kathy's eyes narrowed a moment, then she seemed to realize what she was doing and her face smoothed out, her eyes widening innocently. "We didn't, not really. But he is, was, an important businessman in town. When he saw that the ADA's office was looking for help, he reached out to offer a suggestion. I don't know who was more surprised when he found out I was the ADA and when I found out that he was the one calling."

Nodding, as if she bought the rather thin story, Julie absently played with the gold chain around her neck, partially lifting it from beneath her shirt so some of the distinctive jewels showed.

Kathy went still, her gaze riveted on the jewelry. She cleared her throat and smiled stiffly. "My, what a lovely necklace you're wearing. I don't think I've ever seen anything quite like it."

Julie pulled it the rest of the way out from under her shirt. "It was passed down through my mother's side of the family. I kept it in a safe-deposit box for years along with other family mementos. But after everything that's happened, well, I just want to feel closer to her." She undid the chain and pulled off the necklace. "Then again, I'm told the gems are real. I probably should put it back in the bank to keep it safe."

She crossed to the desk in the front hallway and placed the necklace in the top drawer. "I'll do it tomorrow." She turned around. "Where are my manners? I asked you here for lunch. I doubt a busy attorney like you has a lot of time on her hands. I've got soup and salad waiting in the dining room. Let's enjoy a nice meal and catch up, shall we?"

Kathy took both of Julie's hands in hers. "It really

is good to see you again. I'm so glad you're back. And you're right, I'm starving, and don't have a lot of time. Let's eat."

Julie tugged her hands free, forcing another smile as she led Kathy to the dining room.

Less than an hour later, she stood on the front stoop, waving as Kathy drove away. Then she stepped inside, and into Chris's arms.

"You're shivering." He pulled her close.

"You have no idea how hard it was to sit across from that woman making small talk, knowing all along that she conspired with my husband and my cousin against me. Either way, she had her tracks covered. If Alan had been able to get the necklace, she'd have used that poor woman she'd bribed to have plastic surgery to look like me. Then what? Kill her? Probably. And then kill me of course. Imagine how elated she must feel now, patting herself on the back for keeping my look-a-like alive just in case she could figure out how to use her to get the money, even without the necklace. It must feel like Christmas to her now, seeing me wear that piece of jewelry."

He pulled her back and smiled down at her. "You've baited the trap," he said. "Now, all we have to do is wait."

"There's still so much that could go wrong. That poor woman trusts Kathy. She doesn't know that Kathy will probably kill her as soon as she gets the lump-sum payment."

"We're not going to let that happen. You have to trust me."

She slid her arms up behind his neck. "I do. I trust you. I always have."

He grinned. "Always? Really?"

"Well, okay, maybe not always. It took a few hours."

She kissed him, but all too soon the kiss was over.

"Speaking of a few hours, we don't know how long it will take Kathy to make her move. Go upstairs like we agreed. We'll take it from here."

"Okay. Be careful, Chris. Promise?"

"Promise."

She headed up the winding staircase.

THE BREAK-IN, WHEN it came, was done so swiftly and professionally that the alarm didn't even go off. But Chris and his men were waiting, and watching. And when the burglar handed Julie's necklace through the open limousine window, they followed at a discreet distance.

Assistant district attorney Kathy Nelson was apprehended at the airport, along with a woman who bore an uncanny resemblance to Julie Webb. Chris was astonished at just how alike the two appeared. But the imposter's eyes gave her away. They were dull, a window to a dead soul inside, a woman who'd seen the worst of what life had to offer and had been broken down many years ago and expected nothing better for herself.

After talking to Julie, the woman agreed to take a plea deal and testify against Kathy. In return, she would go under the knife again to get her old face back. That was something that Julie insisted upon. In addition, she'd get the therapy that she needed. And Julie would help her get an apartment and a job, plus provide her a small nest egg to help her start a new life.

The chief thought Julie was crazy to do all of that for a woman who, because she was going to pretend to be Julie, had given Alan, Kathy and her cousin the ability to complete their master plan and then kill Julie to cover their tracks. But Chris understood. Julie was too kindhearted not to help someone who'd been willing to give up her own identity out of desperation for a new life. It was the girl's background that had convinced Julie that she wasn't the hardened criminal the chief thought her to be. The girl was a runaway, had sold herself on the streets just to survive. Julie felt the imposter deserved another chance.

Chris loved that about Julie, that she saw the good in people. That she put others' happiness above her own. She was the kindest woman he'd ever met, and he was deeply in love with her. And that's what made this so damn hard.

He was about to let her go.

As she entered the coffee shop a block from her Nashville home, she looked around for him. She thought he was here to say a temporary goodbye now that the court case was over and he didn't have to testify again. They hadn't talked about long-term plans yet, even though she'd tried to bring it up several times. He'd kept dodging the conversation, knowing she would agree in a heartbeat to move back to Destiny with him. After all, her grandmother was funding Naomi's Hope Foundation now and there was nothing else keeping her here in Nashville.

That had been another surprise to some, that Julie would want to continue the Foundation even though the eventual exhumation had proved that Naomi didn't have an orphan disease. But it didn't surprise Chris. Finding cures for orphan diseases was a cause Julie believed in and she couldn't turn her back on those in need. Apparently, her grandmother agreed. She'd been more than willing to fund the charity.

But she'd decided not to go through with the trust's lump sum payment.

Not without some stipulations, at least. Stipulations that she'd told Chris, but hadn't yet told her granddaughter. Julie was going to find out the terms for herself very soon. And there were about a billion reasons for Julie not to go back to Destiny. Or to Chris.

She just didn't know them yet.

When she saw him, her face lit up and she smiled, as she always did. He watched with a heavy heart as she approached his table. She gave him a quick kiss as he held out her chair for her, a kiss that nearly killed him.

He sat across from her while a waitress took her

order. As soon as the waitress moved away from the table, he pulled the envelope out of his pocket and handed it to her.

"What's this?" she asked.

He pushed his chair back and stood. "It's a letter from your grandmother. I wanted to deliver it in person, make sure that you got it. My cab's waiting out front. I've got to go now. The chief is anxious for me to start a new case."

She frowned. "You're leaving Nashville? Right this minute?"

"Right this minute." Unable to stop himself, he leaned down and kissed her. "Goodbye, Julie."

And then he walked out of the coffee shop, and out of Julie's life forever.

Chapter Twenty-Four

Steaks sizzled on the double-decker grill on Chris's back deck. Once again, Max presided over the cooking. And once again, another young intern from the Destiny Police Department helped him load potatoes and foil-wrapped corncobs onto another section of the grill.

"One week." Dillon grabbed a beer from the cooler at Chris's feet.

Since Dillon was watching Ashley show off her and Dillon's new baby girl, Letha Mae, to half the police force crowding the deck, he wasn't sure what his friend meant.

"One week until what?"

Dillon used his bottle to indicate the intern. "I give this new intern and Max one week. I said two weeks last time and lost the bet."

Chris shrugged and snagged himself a beer. "Looks like we need more ice. I'll get some from the freezer in the garage."

Dillon stopped him with a hand on his shoulder.

"Why don't you just get a ticket and fly to London and sweep Julie off her feet? We're all tired of you moping around like a lovesick calf. It's depressing."

Chris shoved his hand off his shoulder. "A billion dollars, Dillon. Julie's grandmother offered her a billion dollars if she'd agree to live in London with her. And the cherry on top is the old woman wants to pick Julie's next husband. If Julie refuses, she loses all that money. Now you tell me. What woman would give up a billion dollars to marry some redneck cop in Nowhere, Tennessee?"

"This woman would."

Chris froze, then slowly turned. Julie stood at the bottom of the deck stairs, staring up at him. She looked so...damn...good. He hadn't seen her in well over a month, and he couldn't quit drinking her in. God, how he loved her. But, wait, what had she said?

He took a step toward her, then stopped. "What are you doing here?"

She rolled her eyes and marched to the top of the deck. "If that's a proposal, I've heard better. And considering my first husband, that's saying something." She crossed her arms and tapped her shoe.

He took another step toward her, then another, until he was standing right in front of her.

"I didn't think I'd ever see you again."

"Why not?" she asked. "Because you thought I loved money more than I loved you? Seriously? I would think you knew me better than that after everything we've been through. And you should also know that I thought it was wonderfully romantic that my mother and father gave up everything for a future together, and didn't let my grandmother choose who they should love. So why would I, for even one minute, consider letting her choose who I should love?"

By the end of her speech, the deck had fallen silent and she was jabbing him in the chest with her pointer finger.

Chris winced and pulled her hand down. But instead of letting go, he entwined his fingers with hers.

"Can you say that again, please?"

She frowned. "My entire speech? I didn't memorize the darn thing."

"No, just the part where you said you loved me."

Her frown faded, and a smile slowly grew in its place. Then she frowned again. "Wait, that came out all wrong. You're supposed to tell me you love me first. Forget I said that. What I meant to say is that you're too stubborn for your own good and you shouldn't have walked away in that coffee shop. You should have known that, of course, I'd go visit my grandmother, because she is family, after all, and old, and deserved to know about what kind of person Naomi was and—"

"I love you."

She sputtered to a stop in the middle of her sentence. "What did you say?"

"I love you." He framed her face in his hands. "I'm stubborn, stupid and shouldn't have doubted you. I'm sorry. And I love you. And I want to marry you."

He dropped to one knee.

Her mouth fell open and she pressed her hands against her chest.

"No, wait." He stood up. "Wait right here."

He turned around and ran into the house.

JULIE BLINKED AND looked around the deck. What had just happened? Everyone was staring at her, looking just as shocked as she felt. She'd flown from half the world away to get here, fully expecting Chris to beg her forgiveness and ask her to marry him. A little groveling might have been nice, too. Instead, he'd dropped to his knee, then ran away.

Her cheeks flushed hot with embarrassment.

She was about to turn around and slink back to her car when Chris ran out of the house. He stumbled to a halt in front of her and once again dropped to one knee. His face was red and he seemed out of breath, as if he'd run up and down the stairs a few times.

"Julie," he said, between deep breaths, "I need your left hand for this."

She crossed her arms. "I'm not sure I trust you now."

He gave her that irresistible half smile. "Yes, you do. You've always trusted me."

"Well, almost always," she said.

He pulled a black velvet box out from behind his back and opened the lid. A solitaire diamond ring sat in the middle of the plush velvet, sparkling in the sunlight.

She gasped and covered her mouth with her hands.

"It's not very big," he apologized. "But it's the best I could do for now on a cop's salary."

She cleared her throat and lowered her hands. "When...when did you buy that?"

"The day I got out of the hospital. But I wanted all of the loose ends tied up so nothing would stand in our way when I proposed. Then your grandma sent that letter and I thought—"

"You thought wrong."

"I know, I know. I'm trying to fix that now. Julie Elizabeth Webb—"

"Linwood. Julie Elizabeth Linwood. I changed it back to my maiden name."

"Julie Elizabeth Linwood, I love you. Will you do me the honor of becoming my wife?"

In answer, she held out her left hand and smiled so hard her face hurt.

Chris slid the ring onto her finger and stood. "I love you."

"I love you, too."

He swooped down and kissed her.

The deck erupted in applause and laughter as everyone rushed forward to congratulate them.

It was impossible to kiss Chris the way she really wanted to with everyone slapping their backs and telling them how happy they were for them. She broke the kiss, laughing and beaming up at him.

He framed her face in his hands, staring at her in wonder. "I can't believe you gave up all that money to be with me."

"I didn't have a choice," she teased.

"You didn't?"

She shook her head. "It all came down to destiny."

His answering smile filled her heart and soul with happiness. And then he kissed her again, the way a man kisses a woman when he loves her more than life itself, the way a man kisses a woman…when he's found his destiny.

* * * * *

Look for more books in Lena Diaz's miniseries
TENNESSEE SWAT *throughout 2017.*

*You'll find them wherever
Harlequin Intrigue books are sold!*

INTRIGUE

Available February 21, 2017

#1695 HOLDEN
The Lawmen of Silver Creek Ranch • by Delores Fossen
Marshal Holden Ryland needs answers when his ex-flame, Nicky Hart, steals files from the Conceptions Fertility Clinic—but he never expected to uncover a black-market baby ring or risk it all for Nicky and her stolen nephew.

#1696 HOT TARGET
Ballistic Cowboys • by Elle James
Delta Force warrior Max "Caveman" Decker, on loan to Homeland Security, falls victim to desire on assignment protecting Grace Saunders, a sexy naturalist who witnessed a murder in backcountry Wyoming.

#1697 ABDUCTION
Killer Instinct • by Cynthia Eden
FBI Special Agent Jillian West returns home to the Florida coast after working too many tragic cases, but her former lover, navy SEAL Hayden Black, isn't the only man awaiting her return...

#1698 THE MISSING McCULLEN
The Heroes of Horseshoe Creek • by Rita Herron
Cash Koker has always been a loner out of luck, and when he's accused of murder, he has no one to turn to except BJ Alexander, a sexy lawyer ready to put everything on the line to prove her client's innocence.

#1699 FUGITIVE BRIDE
Campbell Cove Academy • by Paula Graves
Security experts Owen Stiles and Tara Bentley are best friends, but their race for survival against terrorists forces them to confront the true depth of their relationship—the passion simmering just below the surface.

#1700 SECRET STALKER
Tennessee SWAT • by Lena Diaz
Former lovers SWAT detective Max Remington and Bexley Kane have a deeply unresolved history between them, but when they're taken captive by gunmen, addressing the past is the only way for them to find a future together.

SPECIAL EXCERPT FROM

*Join FBI agent Craig Frasier and criminal psychologist
Kieran Finnegan as they track down a madman who is
obsessed with perfect beauty.*

"Horrible! Oh, God, horrible—tragic!" John Shaw said,
shaking his head with a dazed look as he sat on his bar
stool at Finnegan's Pub.

Kieran nodded sympathetically. Construction crews
had found old graves when they were working on the
foundations at the hot new downtown venue Le Club
Vampyre.

Anthropologists had found the new body among the
old graves the next day.

It wasn't just *any* body.

It was the body of supermodel Jeannette Gilbert.

Finding the old graves wasn't much of a shock—not in
New York City, and not in a building that was close to two
centuries old. The structure that housed Le Club Vampyre
was a deconsecrated Episcopal church. The church's
congregation had moved to a facility it had purchased
from the Catholic church—whose congregation was now
in a sparkling new basilica over on Park Avenue. While
many had bemoaned the fact that such a venerable old
institution had been turned into an establishment for those
into sex, drugs and rock and roll, life—and business—
went on.

And with life going on…

MEXP1987

Well, work on the building's foundations went on, too.

It was while investigators were still being called in following the discovery of the newly deceased body—moments before it hit the news—that Kieran Finnegan learned about it, and that was because she was helping out at her family's establishment, Finnegan's on Broadway. Like the old church/nightclub behind it, Finnegan's dated back to just before the Civil War, and had been a pub for most of those years. Since it was geographically the closest place to the church with liquor, it had apparently seemed the right spot at that moment for Professor John Shaw.

*A serial killer is striking a little too close to
home in the second novel in the*
NEW YORK CONFIDENTIAL *series,*
A PERFECT OBSESSION
coming soon from New York Times *bestselling author
Heather Graham and MIRA Books.*

$2.00 OFF

New York Times
bestselling author
HEATHER GRAHAM
brings *perfect*
suspense in...
**A PERFECT
OBSESSION**

Available March 28, 2017

Order your copy today!

$26.99 U.S. / $29.99 CAN.

$2.00 OFF the purchase price of A PERFECT OBSESSION by Heather Graham.

Offer valid from March 18, 2017, to September 18, 2017.
Redeemable at participating retail outlets, in-store only. Not redeemable at
Barnes & Noble. Limit one coupon per purchase. Valid in the U.S.A. and Canada only.

52614415

Canadian Retailers: Harlequin Enterprises Limited will pay the face value of this coupon plus 10.25¢ if submitted by customer for this product only. Any other use constitutes fraud. Coupon is nonassignable. Void if taxed, prohibited or restricted by law. Consumer must pay any government taxes. Void if copied. Inmar Promotional Services ("IPS") customers submit coupons and proof of sales to Harlequin Enterprises Limited, P.O. Box 3000, Saint John, NB E2L 4L3, Canada. Non-IPS retailer—for reimbursement submit coupons and proof of sales directly to Harlequin Enterprises Limited, Retail Marketing Department, 225 Duncan Mill Rd., Don Mills, ON M3B 3K9, Canada.

U.S. Retailers: Harlequin Enterprises Limited will pay the face value of this coupon plus 8¢ if submitted by customer for this product only. Any other use constitutes fraud. Coupon is nonassignable. Void if taxed, prohibited or restricted by law. Consumer must pay any government taxes. Void if copied. For reimbursement submit coupons and proof of sales directly to Harlequin Enterprises, Ltd 482, NCH Marketing Services, P.O. Box 880001, El Paso, TX 88588-0001, U.S.A. Cash value 1/100 cents.

5 65373 00082 3   (8100)0 12232

MCOUPHG0217

Turn your love of reading into
rewards you'll love with

Harlequin My Rewards

**Join for FREE today at
www.HarlequinMyRewards.com**

Earn **FREE BOOKS** of your choice.

Experience **EXCLUSIVE OFFERS** and contests.

Enjoy **BOOK RECOMMENDATIONS**
selected just for you.

PLUS! Sign up now
and get **500** points
right away!